THE *Diamond* NECKLACE

THE *Diamond* NECKLACE

TURAB

PARTRIDGE
A Penguin Company

To order additional copies of this book, contact

Partridge India
000 800 10062 62
www.partridgepublishing.com/india
orders.india@partridgepublishing.com

CONTENTS

Love and Understanding
are the STARS of the married life.

They may shine in prosperity
but should dazzle in adversity.

To my wife

Zahara

For 50 years of our Dazzling life

turab

FOREWORD

Turab and I are the same age. We were raised without television and children usually did what was expected of them. In our lifetimes, new social mores and technical inventions drastically changed almost every facet of the human experience. This is a story about adjusting to new perceptions about friendships, marriages and family. How does our traditional generation accept the new, fast-paced one?

Turab has placed his characters in Mumbai, but as an American, I recognize and face the same dilemmas. Readers like us will find very familiar emotions as we try to understand our children. Young readers will recognize the universal need to live out the new norms and relate to the main characters. Turab entertains us with this juxtaposition of value sets, and it is fascinating. Why? "Partly, it's because of their human interest: the fascination of getting to know people who are so similar to us and understandable in some ways, and so unlike us and hard to understand in other ways." (Jared Diamond, <u>The World Until Yesterday</u>)

This story centers around a bona fide friendship between an Indian boy and girl. The lives of the families of these two personable characters intertwine with their lives, and create an interesting slice of life in Mumbai. Turab has described many plausible and current situations that keep the story complex and yet relates back to the main theme. It was rare, when he and I were growing up, for a boy and girl to be close friends. It is not rare now.

Linda Babcock
109 Powderly Court
Folsom, Ca 95630

Business Professor, Santa Monica College
Banker, Retired

CHAPTER 1

Iqbal was nervous on the road awaiting his friend Tabassum to reach. The street filled with people moving around returning home from their work. The street lights just turned on to take the passing stages of sunlight.

With a chewing gum in mouth, he was cursing for having listened to Tabassum and agreed to meet at this time of the hour. Iqbal and Tabassum were staying in the same locality. They have been friends since childhood years. Iqbal had just graduated and Tabassum was in first year of college.

Iqbal saw the sight of Tabassum from a distance, same lovely smiling face with lots of mischief in the eyes. Tabassum was full of energy and always had something new to share with her best friend Iqbal. Tabassum came near and had a book in her hand. Her dress, as expected, dirty and shabby with lots of chocolates marks on the edges indicating her shalwar being used as napkin. Iqbal hated this, but had no way to teach her and stop this habit. His careful mother will not tolerate unworthy manners from him. Iqbal's mother had hard code of conduct and difficult for Tabassum to understand. She teased him and made fun of him. To avenge Iqbal whenever his hands were dirty used the shalwar as napkin to wipe the hands.

Tabassum was—raising her hand and asking him to come to the sweet maker's shop. Iqbal ran to meet her. He was exceedingly fond of sweets.

She was his only source of sweets without the fear of the mother. His mother did not allow him eating sweets at odd times of the day. The mother used to tell him on the disadvantages of too much sweet—which Iqbal never understood and never wanted to understand as long as enjoyed eating sweets. Tabassum bought oily jalebis from the shop, both enjoyed an equal share, and as usual he used her shalwar to clean up the hands and lips.

Iqbal asked why she had called him here and not to her house. She put a finger on her mouth and showed the book to Iqbal.

- I cannot describe this book to you in my house—look what is there, Tabassum said.

Iqbal snatched the book from her hand. On opening, his face flashed, and he shouted,

- What is this? How can you view this book and from where you got it?

The book, with the nude photos of young girls, shocked him.

Tabassum laughed and asked mischievously

- Did you enjoy the photos?

Iqbal shouted

- No, my mom will kill me. She cannot imagine this book in my hand.
- But why should you tell your mom?
- No, I don't tell her.
- They why do you worry?
- But she finds it out?
- How?
- Don't know?
- You are a nut.
- Yes, I am, But from where you got this book?
- It was lying under my father's pillow. I saw and wanted to show you with mischief on her smile.
- To me for what?
- Why don't you enjoy? You are a liar. Let me go now. I have to put the book there before he comes home. Tabassum wanted to grab the book from Iqbal's hand and run, but Iqbal hold her hand.

The feelings of holding her hand now was different and as if a spasm passed through his body. Iqbal looked at the book few more pages—few more nude photos—the pictures were now of Tabassum, and the revolting feelings in his mind confused him. But Tabassum snatched the book from his hand and ran away—lots of smiles, strange feelings and left him in his wondrous world.

CHAPTER 2

Iqbal reached home, and as usual the mother asked.

- Where were you and why so late?
- With Tabassum, he just blurted out.
- Again with her? She has nothing do but loiter here and there.
- What were you doing?

Iqbal lost nerves. Does the mother know?

- Nothing mom had few jalebis.
- Again sweets?—How much sweets she eats in the whole day?—have you seen her? How much fat she is?
- No mom, not fatty at all
- How can you judge? Look at her, she is more than what she should be at her age

Seeing body—Oh God, This shocked Iqbal. Why Tabassum's body? I am sure she knows the truth as always and is testing.

Iqbal wanted to laugh, but the face was betraying.

- Ok go and wash face. It is now time for prayers.

A convenient excuse to run and he obeyed his instincts.

Tabassum on reaching home found father's voice discussing something with mom.

Tabassum became nervous and hide the book in the shalwar.

- But I have seen it, the father was saying.

The words were a thunder storm for Tabassum—What will she do now?

- We have to be careful before any action, the mother said.
- Yes, I agree, but cannot neglect. You don't get decent boys now days, and Ashraf is an excellent boy. The family is rich, and they like our daughter.

Tabassum ran fast into the father's room and locked the door.

- Look what you did? The mother shouted, she overheard the talk, ran away and locked the room.

Once inside the room Tabassum had a high relief, threw her on the bed.

Tabassum guessed what parents were talking. That Ashraf is an idiot—if he has money, so what? But first hide the book. That was the priority.

Tabassum thanked God for helping and saving her from the disgrace. She took a personal oath not to do this idiotic behaviour in future.

But what she can do! Iqbal, being always on her mind.

She had to share the same. But now she has to resolve this problem.

She wanted to cry but held the emotions.

The knock on the door alerted her. The mother knocked and asked to open the door. She opened and ran into the welcoming arms of mother.

- I want to study—go to college and become a doctor, the words just came.
- Yes, my dear, dad does not want to throw away this opportunity. It is a loving family, and we know the boy. Meet him and then decide.
- But I don't want to meet, She just shouted and revolted.

This jolted the mother. The father shouted at highest pitch—What!

- We have checked everything. You should check too, if you want.
- I don't want to, she continued her revolt.
- Once you meet—you will understand better

The mother tried to console her.

- I don't want to meet him, mom, please.

The father wanted to say something, but the mother intervened and took Tabassum in the next room.

The father went to room and saw the disturbed pillow.

He assumed Tabassum has used it to hide the cries.

But when saw the edge of the book, he got shocked. He lifted the pillow, the book was there.

His mind went into dizziness. How did the book come here? He had no clue—had he left there?—Forgotten?—Has Tabassum seen?—If so what is she thinking? Has he lost the respect as father?

His mind blocked, he had no answers.

He sat on the chair holding face with both hands.

The mother, Zaheda came and saw her husband, sitting on the chair.

- Don't worry and get excited. I will make her understand.

Hamid could not lift his hands and face Zaheda, his wife.

He moaned and said,

- Yes, indeed you will, my dear.

He had no courage to tell Zaheda what he was suffering.

- It is now time for the prayers, and you wish to go to mosque or not?

Yes, Yes, Hamid jumped from chair. Allah can help to come out of this predicament—Has Tabassum seen the book?

He heard the sound of Azan. It was prayer time. Hamid got up and went to the mosque. After the prayer, on the way, he met Inayatullah, the sweet meat shop owner.

- How are you? Inayatullah inquired.
- By the grace of Allah, I am fine.
- Your one postcard is at the shop please take it.
- My postcard! Why postman has, given it to you?
- No, Tabassum came to shop to buy jalebi, and must have fallen from the book. I saw after she left.

The shop came, and Inayatullah gave the postcard to him.

On seeing the postcard, Hamid became nervous . . . How this postcard is here. It was in that book.

His voice crumbled, but asked.

- When did she come?
- Half an hour ago—she and Iqbal came.
- Iqbal, who is Iqbal?
- Iqbal, the son of Sharifa

Hamid's strength crumbled—felt dizziness—and sat on the chair. The blood flow from the body froze.

- Are you alright?—a shocked Inayatullah asked
- Get a glass of water, please.
- Abdul go and get a glass of water.

Hamid drank water, but eyes become wet. He could not control the emotions.

He started walking but was shaking.

- Hamid, you are not well—should I drop you home?
- No, thanks, have the problem of blood pressure.

He started walking, his mind now shattered.

First Tabassum and now Iqbal.

What should he do? How to face Tabassum? Allah has given a tremendous punishment for doing something against the dictates of HIS commands. A father of a growing daughter should control himself. How idiotic it was to bring the book home and have intimate time with wife. He cursed himself and cursed his friend Imdad, who gave the book. But then the conscious revolted, it was his fault, his weakness and Allah was punishing him.

He entered the house. Zaheda was in the kitchen. Tabassum opened the door and looked at the condition of father. A smiling—welcoming—hugging father was missing.

- Are you alright dad?"

Zaheda heard this and came running.

- What happened?—are you alright?—Please tell. Should I call the doctor? Did you fight with someone?

A series of questions from a worried wife!

- No, I am alright; will rest for a while, mumbled Hamid.

Nervous Tabassum thought—is it because of her? She was shocked that her refusal of Ashraf could be so devastating for her father.

She went inside and sat next to him, holding his hand. Hamid could not control himself and hugged her. His eyes were wet and had an apologetic face.

- Papa, I love you and do what you say, she said crying.

The words flowed by itself. She had no control over it.

Hamid was uncomfortable—holding her hand—his eyes wide open and looked at his daughter. He felt that he had to fulfil her wish and make her happy.

- Yes, my dear I know it.
- You please go to sleep, Zaheda uttered and asked Tabassum to go in the kitchen and prepare dal which was on the stove.

Tabassum went; Hamid closed eyes and went to sleep.

Zaheda checked the forehead to see if he had any fever. She knew her husband well and thought that Tabassum's refusal must have upset him. It was normal, and nothing to worry. She closed the light and went out.

CHAPTER 3

Iqbal had a disturbed night, and just could not sleep.

Why did Tabassum show the photos?

Was this a mistake, mischief, intention or the reason?

This kept him tense and wide awake.

Iqbal heard mother's voice

- Why still awake—go to sleep?

- Reading a book and will try to sleep once finished, Mom, go to sleep.

He picked up a book and opened it, in case, she walks in the room.

But, she switched off room light, and Iqbal moaned a sigh of relief.

Tabassum haunted him. He wanted to ask her but how?

How to start the conversation with her when she meets him in the morning?

Will she be ashamed of what she has done?

What will she say on the book and her intentions?

Iqbal closed the eyes. Tabassum was there as imagined in one of the photos and wanted to touch her.

Suddenly the photo become active—she was there now moving. Same mischievous smile on face, which she had at the time of showing the book.

Iqbal could not resist and ran to catch her, wanted to kiss and show his love.

Holding face in both the hands, he kissed her.

He did not find any resistance but sensed the full warmth of her lips wanting to be kissed.

He pressed her with intensity and in that vigorous shifting; his legs hit the side table which fell on the floor creating a thundering sound.

-   What happened Iqbal?

It was mother's voice. Sharifa had switched on the lights.

This shocked him His physical stature being difficult; he cannot accept his mother in that condition.

Iqbal ran to bathroom, shouting,

-   Nothing happened mom—just hit the table while sleeping and it fell.

Sharifa will not accept this. She knew her son being a sound sleeper, and she had taught him even the sleeping manners. He cannot hit any table while sleeping. She entered the room, switched on the light.

Iqbal in the bathroom, the bed in a mess, the pillows scattered. This shocked her. These were not the sleeping manners which she had taught him.

She knew the water is running in the bath. Is Iqbal having a bath at this time of night? Confused but not an idiot, she realised, her son had now become a man.

With the content on her face—she closed the light, closed the door and went away.

Iqbal sensed the closing of the door and heaved a sigh of relief. He opened the bathroom door and saw no lights in the room.

He came out changed the clothes and tried to sleep. With a different feeling, he dozed off into his normal sleep.

Sharifa blushed once inside her room. She never realised her son being a grown up man. It was her mission now to think of his marriage and find a decent girl for him.

The thoughts rushing to her mind.

In her visualisation, they were

Zarina—the daughter of his father's sister.

Zeenat—the daughter of her friend Nisreen

Zubeda—the grand-daughter of her uncle.

She laughed and laughed—the choice being much wider.

Tabassum was nowhere in her thoughts.

CHAPTER 4

Iqbal's mother Sharifa, from a religious middle class family, had a disciplined and contented childhood. At the age of ten, she finished her first lesson of the Quran. She learned the essential skills which a woman is supposed to know to become a devoted wife and a responsible mother.

Masood, her father a Maulvi and a school teacher gave her essential training and education. Maimuna, her mother from a small primitive village had not much education. But she was a loving mother and a never demanding wife. Self-contention and a strong belief in Allah and HIS Mercy were her strong beliefs.

Sharifa's education was limited to the school level. She with natural talent and the grasping power—a strong characteristic of her father learnt fast. Once she attained her puberty age, she stopped going to school and confined to the house.

Sharifa used to read the books of his father. Following the books with much ease and whenever she had any questions she asked the father who took interest in the quest and satisfied her.

Once she asked a stupid question.

- Dad what is the difference between God and Allah.

Father laughed.

- You are too young to understand it, but let me explain. They are the same thing and one Entity. God is a word to express that entity. Allah is the same entity but has feelings included in the name. Allah has other ninety nine names which expresses those feelings and characters of him.
- He can love you, can punish you, and can forgive you.

- She was happy to hear that.
- See I am your father, he continued, "I love you, punish you, and I take care of you, but I am still the same one person."
- But you only punish me, she said mischievously

The father hugged her, and they both laughed.

At the age of fifteen, she understood the meaning of life more in deep . . .

Sharifa at other occasion asked another question to her mother.

- How come Allah has given all the benefits of life to a man and left the woman to have only sufferings."

The mother smiled.

- You are mistaken my dear—The definition of benefits and sufferings are not to be taken in the worldly sense. The benefits are the sufferings and sufferings are the benefits in the definitions of Allah. Why Allah says that the Jannat is under the feet of mother and not father? Why Allah gave this great honour to mother because mother is the symbol of sufferings.

The mother continued.

- Look at the history of mankind. Study and explore the history of Islam. Allah has always given sufferings to his beloved ones and not the worldly benefits, which you are thinking.

This touched her with deep intensity . . . She resolved that when Allah blesses her with the motherhood, she will be the best Mother.

She grew up with this. At the age of eighteen, a marriage proposal came through her father's cousin, who gave an excellent reference of the boy. Masood accepted because of the strong recommendation and trust in the cousin. The family was small. Father took her consent, and she married to Abdullah.

She moved with Abdullah to Mumbai where he worked as a salesman with a local shoe store.

Abdullah's family had an aged mother and a sister. His father expired two years ago due to Malaria which sprayed in the city and proved fatal.

This created financial difficulties for the family as now Abdullah's paltry income was not able to cope with the expenses.

Sharifa's life became now demanding. She had no financial worries at father's house. Whatever she needed was available to her by the loving parents.

It was difficult for her to run the house with limited income. Abdullah used to give money to his mother to keep the house hold expenses but now the mother insisted that Abdullah gives this responsibility to Sharifa.

Sharifa had to find another source of income and as knowledge of Qur'an being her only asset, she thought of giving private tuitions to the children. With the consent of Abdullah, she spread the message, started teaching and created extra income.

While teaching Qur'an, she mixed up well with children. They were around the age of five. These children made her to think about her own child. She started imagining. She was teaching to her own child.

Allah, blessed her with the good news one day, and she was pregnant. There was happiness in the family on hearing the news of her pregnancy.

Iqbal was born after three years of her marriage.

CHAPTER 5

Hamid woke up early than usual time and but felt tired because of disturbed sleep. Zaheda, preparing the breakfast and Tabassum reading news paper.

The book haunted Hamid. The question in mind—Had Tabassum seen the book? Had Iqbal seen the book? Had they seen the book together? How to find out and if so what to do? Hamid wanted to see Tabassum and assess if she had any reaction.

Tabassum looked at Hamid, smiled and asked,

How are you dad?

Feeling alright?

Slept well?

Remembered me in your prayers?

- Her usual questions with full jest of life. No change, no guilt feelings.
- Tabassum's routine behaviour convinced Hamid that she must not have seen the book.

But the postcard? Surely was in that book. How it reached the shop of Inayatullah? He murmured, something must be wrong somewhere?

Hamid decided to meet Iqbal and check how Iqbal behaves. But before that he wanted to test Tabassum . . .

- What Iqbal is doing? Hamid inquired.
- I don't know dad—he has just finished finals and waiting for the result. Dad he is brilliant and helps everyone in studies. He is a dear friend.
- Yes, I am aware—ask him to meet me, maybe I can help him to get a decent job.

- Will you dad?—Tabassum jumped from the seat.

The excitement and joy seen in her body confused Hamid and scared him . . .

Zaheda called from the kitchen and asked them to come for the breakfast.

She noticed the excitement on the face of her daughter and asked.

- Why are you so happy? Did you get something from your father? What is it?
- Nothing mom, dad is going to help Iqbal to get a suitable job

Zaheda looked at Hamid.

She as a woman guessed what was in her husband's mind.

He was thinking of Ashraf, and Iqbal tormented him.

- That is courteous of him. They are poor people, and if we can help them, Allah will bless us.
- They are not so poor mom—they live happily.

The thought of her mother that they are poor had to be fought back.

- Sharifa aunt is so polite and takes care of the house so well. She is alone but manages everything in the house.
- Mom you have no idea. How much trouble she has taken for Iqbal's education. If dad can help them, Allah will bless him.

This closeness of Tabassum shocked Hamid.—Oh! Does she know so much? She knows them so well. I must meet Iqbal and give him a proposal. A respectable job and get out of Tabassum's life. Their friendship made him more uncomfortable.

Though not sure whether Iqbal has seen the book, he decided to meet him. He made his decision. Iqbal has to get out from here and the life of his daughter.

- Tabbu, tell Iqbal—I want to meet him. Today evening after I come back from office.
- I will tell him.

Her excitement was clearly visible . . .

Zaheda confused, and worried.

What are the real intentions of her husband?

CHAPTER 6

After Iqbal's birth—Sharifa's health was not keeping well. Sharifa could not sustain the added burden of the tuitions and had to stop. This reduced income and created more financial difficulties. The aged mother could not help. The young sister-in-law, Shabana would not help.

Sharifa's father—Masood visited and could visualize the difficult condition. Masood asked Abdullah if Sharifa comes to his house, he can look after treatment. Abdullah expressed hesitancy because of mother's health, and Sharifa was needed at the house. Masood suggested employing a domestic help so that Sharifa's health could be taken care. This was not possible but Abdullah was reluctant.

Masood wanted to take Sharifa and insisted that she comes with him. Masood even suggested that Abdullah should take leave and come with the whole family and this will solve all the problems . . .

Abdullah's pride did not accept this. Abdullah could not avail leave from the shop because of salary deduction. This was not desirable and he finally agreed. Iqbal's concern in mind, Sharifa decided to go and leave Abdullah alone.

Sharifa left with Masood. The fresh air, loving care of mother and father helped to recover faster. Iqbal enjoyed grand-parents love and affection.

A week had passed, and Abdullah's call came. The Mother has expired, and Sharifa should return. Masood and Maimuna left for Mumbai with Sharifa.

Sharifa blamed herself for the death of mother-in-law.

Masood tried to comfort, but it did not help.

On reaching Mumbai, the condition became still worse. The religious rites of burial and fateha finished by the time they reached Mumbai.

Abdullah's response was arrogant. He treated Sharifa as if she had killed mother. Masood could not tolerate this, and tried to pacify Abdullah. It was Allah's grace that, HE took away his mother in HIS attention and relieved her of physical sufferings. Abdullah being difficult and stubborn did not help Masood much. Masood finally had to go back

On the departure day, Masood reminded Sharifa that the sufferings bestowed by Allah gave the mental courage and to stay stead fast in her behaviour. Masood told if she needs any financial support she should ask him. Masood parted with a heavy heart. Sharifa had decided not to cry. She kept inner strength in control. Once they had gone, and alone, she cried and cried.

Iqbal aged five started the school. Shabana was going to madressah. Iqbal started the initial years in madressah. Sharifa wanted to admit Iqbal in best school to have a formal education. There was not enough money to support the expenses of both the child.

Sharifa asked Abdullah
- I want to send Iqbal to an English School
- You are aware I cannot afford it so don't talk. He will continue his madressah.
- To manage expenses, I will get the extra work. This is the need of the time. I will give him proper education.
- If you can take care of it then acceptable. Don't ask me for more money. I am tired of this life. I wished my blessed mother had found the rich girl and solved my problems.

Sharifa had to digest this insult. Her commitment and issues being different remained silent. Iqbal's education was priority; she had decided to seek father's advice, but needed Abdullah's approval.
- Dad knows the charitable Trusts, and if you agree I will ask and he will find the way to help.
- No, we don't need financial support from him.
- We are not taking his money. It is the trust's funds, and trusts are made for this purpose. The good souls, who have been blessed with wealth, create these trusts and use it for charitable purposes.
- There are so many children loitering on the road without education. Why your father is not helping them?

One more insult, but determined to get approval.

- It is not in his hands. Trust gives money to the deserving candidates for education.
- Then arrange for Shabana too so that we can admit her in English school.
- Shabana is dull, and her school reports are not suitable. I don't think Trust will accept the proposal. But I will still try.
- What will people say? My son goes to English school and sister to madressah. I cannot accept this. The Trust has to support both.

Iqbal is a boy; needs education and has to progress in life. Shabana has to get a formal education and become a devoted house wife. I was educated in madressah. It is good enough for girls.

- Yes, I experienced how talented you are as wife? Don't teach lessons. Do what you want. I am fed up with life.

Sharifa thanked Allah for the help and approval of her husband.

She contacted Masood and requested him to get the funds for both Iqbal and Shabana.

Masood was happy. He agreed with Sharifa that formal education was essential. It was the need of the day. He will try and get funds from the Trust. World is changing at much faster pace, and we have to keep pace with it.

Masood had excellent contacts with the Trustees who respected him for his helping nature. Getting the necessary funds for both Iqbal and Shabana was difficult. Shabana's reports were not convincing. The comment, that she is not responsible, has not finished reading of Q'uran at the age of 10 being most disturbing. Iqbal's excellent reports indicated his brilliant performance and ability to absorb the subjects. It mentioned his superb memory and retentivity.

Masood with the significant efforts managed to convince the trustees and allot funds for both of them. They obliged him but imposed yearly review as a condition

Iqbal and Shabana got enrolled in an English School. Iqbal admitted in the Fourth Std. Shabana admitted in the Ninth Std.

The life moved at its own pace. Iqbal's brilliant performance in school pleased Sharifa.

Sharifa's marriage life as hard as before with increasing financial difficulties, every day there were arguments and quarrels.

- We should not speak harsh in front of our children, she said to Abdullah.
- It is you who is creating this trouble in the house.

- What am I doing? I am not looking after the house but doing more household duties so that our children can get a decent life, and we can satisfy their desires.
- So what? Your responsibility? I am not asking you to work. I am asking you to live with what I earn.
- But that is not enough for us.
- Nothing is enough in life. A dutiful wife has to learn how to survive in the husband's income. You are always demanding more and more. You have no idea of my struggle.
- World is changing. We can't deny our children. Their expectations are changing. You have no idea how much Shabana is now demanding, wants formal dresses every day and taunts me that I don't care for her.
- She speaks the truth. For you, everything is Iqbal. She is nobody to you.
- How can you say that? I have always treated her as my daughter and have always treated her well. On the contrary, she does not treat me well. You are her brother, and your duty to talk to her.
- You don't teach me what I am supposed to do as an elder brother.
- If you don't do it, we will regret it one day.
- I am tired of life. I don't know what am I supposed to do?
- Do your prayers and ask for Allah's blessing. You don't even offer your prayers in time, and you even don't pray. It is not acceptable.

Abdullah lost his temper and wanted to slap Sharifa. He even raised his hand, but the sparkle in the eyes of Sharifa stopped him. His hand trembled, and he went away.

The feud and arguments being watched by Shabana through the open door. Sharifa had asked both Iqbal and Shabana to bed and convinced that the children had gone to sleep. Iqbal had gone to sleep, but Shabana woke up and heard the argument between the two. She aged fourteen started to understand the meaning of life.

Shabana was developing a dislike of Sharifa

CHAPTER 7

Iqbal's school progress made Sharifa happy . . . The school's regulations wanted parents to sign the reports, and Abdullah never bothered signing. Sharifa signed the reports for both Iqbal and Shabana.

Shabana's reports were poor. The performance in class not up to the mark and even the Trust officials warned that if she does not improve, it may not be possible to extend the allocation of trust funds.

Sharifa used to ask Iqbal to do Shabana's home work too. This was hard for Iqbal due to Shabana being in the higher class, yet he still tried. The training gave an added advantage of learning the things beyond his class and improved his skills and created an envious situation in class.

The classmates were always jealous and one of them decided to play tricks. He stole Iqbal's report register before the day of submission to the class teacher.

When time came to deposit the register, Iqbal could not find it. He searched everywhere, but it was not there. The class teacher asked to search at home.

Sharifa had trained him to take care of things and be an organised child. He was nine by that time but knew responsibilities well. The register was in bag when he had come to the school. Mom had signed and kept in the bag.

Iqbal reached home and told Sharifa about the loss of register. This disturbed them. They searched the house but could not find. Sharifa knew that Iqbal will get first rank in the class. She felt it must be in the class, or a stupid child destroyed it.

Sharifa's strength was her prayers. She was sure that prayers will be answered, and the register will be found.

Next day she gave the encouragement to Iqbal and taught a short prayer to recite on entering the class.

Iqbal followed the instructions of mother.

In the first period of Arithmetic, the class teacher asked Iqbal to come and do a calculation on the board. Iqbal went to the board and started solving the sum. While writing, the left hand touched the surface of the board and the board moved. Something dropped from behind the board. It was the register.

He could not believe it, and was so happy. The teacher surprised to see the register, and realised that it must be the mischief of the jealous student, and looked at the children, few clapped, few silent—Thomas was not looking at the board. He suspected but did not want to make an issue. When the result declared, Iqbal indeed stood first. He wished Iqbal well.

Iqbal's mind had a strong impact of this incident. He remembered mother's faith in the prayers.

Iqbal's belief in the prayer was taking deep root in moulding of his personality and character. Sharifa's image and respect were a source of the mental strength.

On reaching home, he narrated the whole incident to mother. Sharifa thanked Allah for answering prayers, and took this opportunity to imbibe in Iqbal a strong belief in prayers.

CHAPTER 8

The financial difficulties had forced Sharifa to opt for other domestic work. Cooking being her strong point, she looked for families needing this help. Sharifa was introduced to Zaheda by her friend. Zaheda was sick and confined to bed, needed help. One day Iqbal came along with Sharifa to Zaheda's house and met Tabassum, Zaheda's daughter. And they became friends.

Tabassum had lot of games to play which, Iqbal never saw or played. This became a powerful attraction for him to come to her house and play. Zaheda first did not wanted her domestic servant's son to play with her, but as she understood Iqbal, she found him a decent mannered child and more intelligent than her daughter. She developed a liking for Sharifa as the cooking was delicious.

The childhood of both taking a deeper root of intimacy. Tabassum always mischievous—Iqbal always innocent, teased, tormented and tumbled by her. They grew up together with the innocence of childhood.

In June, Sharifa received a call from her friend Nisreen that her father and mother met with an accident, and she should come soon.

Sharifa was shattered. She contacted Abdullah at work and gave him the sad news.

Sharifa wanted to leave at once, but Abdullah not able to arrange the funds. He was in debts, and knew well that raising more funds was not possible for him.

Sharifa had no choice. She came to Zaheda and asked for the help and explained the urgency. With sympathies and after consoling, Zaheda gave Rs. 2000/—which she had.

Sharifa left with Iqbal for the native town. Abdullah could not go because of work in the shop. The employer did not grant the leave. Throughout the journey, she prayed, cried and Iqbal consoled her.

On reaching home, she came to realize that the situation was worst then the information she had. The parents were on a visit to a friend's son wedding in a bus. The heavy rains and the bus fallen off the bridge. Six people died on the scene and her parents injured, serious and admitted to hospital.

Mother, Maimuna still unconscious

Father, Masood had multiple injuries, but visitors were permitted.

Sharifa first went to the unconscious mother. She looked at her face. It was the face full of serenity. Sharifa unable to control the emotions started crying. Iqbal held her hand and cried too. Nisreen tried to comfort her, but it was not possible.

- Uncle wants to meet you, she said
- Yes,

Sobbing Sharifa just could not utter anything.

Nisreen led her to the next room near Masood's bed. The visitors saw Sharifa and made room for her to be near Masood. Sharifa unable to control herself cried intensively. Masood looked at Sharifa. He was bruised, wounded and the broken leg held in plaster. With eyes open, he just glanced. The eyes were telling something to Sharifa which she understood. He was inquiring about Maimuna. He tried to speak but unable to utter an audible word. Sharifa raised Iqbal and showed him. For the first time, he was seeing his grand-son after four years. The shine in his eyes indicated his inner happiness on seeing Iqbal.

Nisreen's husband Ali standing nearby approached Sharifa and made her aware of the situation. The drunk driver lost control of the bus due to heavy rains and poor visibility. The bus fell from the bridge. Three hours later, the help reached the place and people rescued. Six people died on the spot. Many were severely injured and unconscious. He tried to comfort Sharifa. The visiting hours were over, and they had to leave the hospital. Doctors were still not sure of Maimuna as she was in a coma and they were trying their best. The hospital was not equipped with the best amenities as it was in the village. Doctors were of the opinion to wait for tonight. If no improvement, than to shift her to the city hospital.

Nisreen asked Sharifa to come to their house and stay with them. Sharifa insisted that she will stay at the hospital, and they take Iqbal to their house.

Hospital authorities agreed to let her stay with her father. Nisreen left with Iqbal.

Masood with heavy dose of sedatives went to sleep. Sharifa sat next to his bed, prayed in the night for their speedy recovery. It was a difficult time for her too. The tiresome journey and the stress of the event took its toll. She had strong moral courage and a spiritual mindset. She just kept on praying and kept herself soaked in the recital of Q'uran, her foundation of strong faith.

CHAPTER 9

Next day morning, Masood opened eyes, saw Sharifa sitting near feet. Their eyes met, and hearts talked to each other. Sharifa went near the head and wanted to talk . . . Masood was not able to speak, and this was more torturing for Sharifa. She never wanted to tell that mother was in a coma and doctors were going to transfer her today in the city hospital.

The nurse came to give medicine to Masood.

- How is mother, she inquired?
- I do not know. She is in the different ward.
- Can I go and meet?
- Yes, if the nurse there permits.

Sharifa waved at Masood indicating that she is going to visit the mother. She got permission through the eyes of Masood.

Sharifa started walking towards the ward. On reaching there, observed impulsive movement of the nurses and the doctor. A cloud of dizziness took over the control of her body. She was about to fall, and one nurse caught hold of her. She made her sat on the chair and gave a glass of water . . .

- How is the mother? Sharifa screamed.

Nurse was silent . . .

- Please talk to me. How is she? Her voice was trembling.

The doctor came. He realised Sharifa's condition, took her hand and wanted to check the pulse. The pulse rate had reduced. He ordered a glass of water and asked the nurse to give two pills to Sharifa.

- No, I do not need any medicine. I want to see mother.

The intensity of her voice was hysterical.

Doctor took both her hands in his hands.

- She has died in peace. Pray for her . . . . , He could not complete the sentence.

Sharifa went into a deep silence. She looked at everyone present in the room. Her silence from the state of trembling and shouting was a surprise to everyone. The nurse came with a glass of water and two tablets. Doctor requested her to take the medicine. She took the medicine, and sat on the chair dumb founded. The tears had dried all of a sudden. The face was radiating rays of the rising sun. It looked as if a miracle has happened, and a divine power has taken over the control of her body and mind. With the courage, Sharifa spoke and asked for Nisreen and Ali. She asked that uncle Hussain should be informed.

Nisreen and Ali came on hearing the news. Nisreen was crying. Ali was trying to calm Sharifa.

- Uncle, now we have to decide for the funeral and fateha.—A controlled Sharifa said?
- Yes, indeed, I will take care. Masood may not be able to bear it.
- But . . . .

And he stopped.

- What is it? Uncle you were trying to say something and stopped.
- No, we have to inform Abdullah too.
- Yes, I will tell, but he may not be able to come at once. We have to complete the funeral as early as possible. That is the commandment of Allah . . .
- Yes, you are right but . . . .

And he stopped.

- Do not worry about the funeral cost. I know it. At present, I will need your help. Uncle Hussain will be arriving soon. I will talk to father and will arrange for the same.
- No, No do not worry about it.

Ali realised the controlled and dignified conduct of Sharifa, took the responsibility and got busy in completing hospital formalities and the funeral arrangement.

Sharifa informed Abdullah.

The most disturbing task was how to tell Masood. After much thinking, Sharifa decided to meet Masood and prayed to Allah to give him the strength to bear it. Sharifa prayed for the same strength. She felt it was given to her by HIM.

She went near to Masood. His eyes were wide awake. Sharifa's face did not reveal anything to him. He tried to raise his hand. Sharifa went near to him, took his hand in her hand and kissed it. The warmth of her kiss gave him inner strength.

Sharifa took a piece of paper and just wrote a couplet in Arabic. It was the couplet prayed for the departed soul.

The father read it, understood it that his wife left him and departed from this world. He was numbed. Sharifa holding his hand felt as if the blood was freezing. Both of them locked in the emotions of a life time. Sharifa decided she will not cry and give all the strength to her father.

Ali came to meet them. The body needed to be taken to the mosque for the final funeral arrangements, and they have to leave the hospital. Sharifa kissed father and took permission to leave through eye contact.

CHAPTER 10

Funeral performed with dignity. The mosque was full of people indicating the love towards the departed soul. As the day was about to end, Sharifa went to the hospital again with Iqbal, and carried a small quantity of soil from the grave for Masood to recite Maimuna's death prayer. With the soil in hand, Masood recited the final prayer.

Nisreen wanted Sharifa and Iqbal to stay at their house. Sharifa insisted to go to Masood's house, but requested to take Iqbal for the night. Nisreen agreed and dropped Sharifa to Masood's house.

On the way, Nisreen gave the house key and the other keys which the hospital authorities had given. Sharifa could recognize the house and cupboards keys. Nisreen also gave two bangles removed from Maimuna's hand. Nisreen informed that the luggage still not found by the police. Nobody knows what it contained.

On entering the house, Sharifa found it clean and tidy as mother always maintained. In the bedroom while staring, the emotions gave way. The flow of tears was unstoppable. Waiting for loneliness, and not to be disturbed by anyone, she just cried, cried and cried till eyes, body and mind tired. She sat on the floor and did not remember when sleep took over her body.

The morning Azan woke her. Sharifa finished prayers. Somebody knocked on the door. Fatema, the next door neighbour had come with tea and bread. Sharifa hugged, accepted condolence and thanked for the breakfast.

Nisreen called to find out if she had slept well and will come for the breakfast.

- How is Iqbal? Did he behave well?

- Oh he is an adorable boy. Zeenat wanted to play with him, but he refused. He was quiet and tensed. He was no problem. He inquired and wanted to meet you.
- Yes, I will come; Fatema has come with the breakfast. I will still come and eat breakfast with him. He is used to eating breakfast with me.
- Ali will come and pick you up, then.
- Fine I will be ready.

Ali came to take her. On the way, they talked about Masood's health and recovery. The doctors were saying the healing will take its own time. Sharifa wanted to go to the city hospital for better analysis and treatment, but decided to listen to Ali and doctor's advice.

On reaching home, Iqbal and Zeenat came running to her. She hugged both of them. Nisreen had the breakfast ready.

After the breakfast—it was time to go to the bus stop to get Abdullah.

- I will go and get him, Ali said.
- Will you bring him home? Sharifa asked
- It depends on him. I will ask him.
- I think you bring him home. Let him get fresh. You leave me at home on the way.
- I will pack the breakfast for you and give you milk so that he can have his breakfast, Nisreen said.
- It is not required, he must have had it on the way, Sharifa said.
- Fine that is ok then but you have lunch with us.
- Insha'Allah, she said.

They both left, Ali dropped them on the way and went to the bus stop to pick up Abdullah.

CHAPTER 11

The bus arrived in time. Abdullah came with Shabana. He had taken a week's break from the shop. On the way, Ali made him aware and explained what happened.

Abdullah listened without any reactions. On reaching home, Sharifa inquired if they need any breakfast. Shabana was hungry and had the breakfast, Abdullah said no.

Ali took them first to Maimuna's grave and offered prayers, and then went to the hospital to see Masood. Masood just waved hand. Abdullah had no words to speak.

Sharifa had gone to the doctor to inquire the progress of Masood and when could be taken home. Doctor said, it may be a week or so to remove the bandage as the broken leg bone will be healed by that time. Masood still may not be able to walk but can use the wheel chair. It may take a month or two for the leg to recover and give the necessary strength to walk.

This worried Sharifa more. Who will look after him? She made up her mind to take Masood to Mumbai. Will Abdullah agree? This will no doubt add to the financial burden. Sharifa decided that maybe she will to do more work. Masood will be most disturbed that her daughter was doing domestic work of which he was not aware. Will he agree?

Many unanswered questions!

Many ambiguities of life!

The loss of Sharifa's mother was a tremendous blow.

Next day morning after breakfast, Sharifa asked Abdullah

- What we should do now? We need the money for daily expenses.

- I have no extra money. They gave Rs. 1000 from the shop as an advance, because of the death in the family. You know how difficult for me.
- The funeral expenses are incurred by Nisreen's husband and I don't know how much. I ask and pay him.
- I am sure, Masood has lots of money, and will take care when returns from hospital. Ali can wait for few days you don't worry.
- Yes, I am sure; he has funds to take care. But still worried.
- Worried for what?
- I want to take him home with us. He is alone, and life will be difficult for him.
- Oh how that is possible, we have no place in the house.
- You are right, but we can offer our room to him. You sleep in the gallery; I and Iqbal can sleep in the kitchen. It is a matter of days. Or I stay here, and you can take care of Iqbal. Iqbal has to go to school, and he should not miss school.
- No, I cannot manage Iqbal, you have no idea how much work is there, and cannot look after him.
- If you wish, stay here with Iqbal.
- But the school is essential.
- Why school is so serious, let him miss. I missed schools so many days. My father wanted me to work in the shop; he did not send me to school and took me to work in the shop.
- The days have changed. If he misses school, he will miss lessons. His progress and the record will suffer.
- So what—he is not going to become a lawyer or a doctor. Once school is over he has to work and help me. He has to earn and feed family. As I have been doing.
- No, that is not the future of Iqbal; I will not let it happen. I will educate him. I want him to become an engineer. He is our future.
- Do not have ambitious dreams for your son. Understand the realities of life. Don't be an idiot.
- Let us not argue. I will talk to father and see what he has to say. I am getting ready to go the hospital. Are you coming with me?

Sharifa left the room, and prepared a cup of coffee for Masood, who liked the coffee prepared by her. It was more than four years; she had not prepared the coffee for him.

- Is Ali going to come to take us to the hospital, Abdullah asked?

- No, we will go by bus. It is not far away, and we cannot bother him. He has his own work to do.
- So what—we are guest, he can take care.
- What! We are not guest. We are here to take care of family.

Abdullah's reasoning was beyond her comprehension. She stopped talking and went to get Iqbal ready.

They reached the hospital. On reaching, she learnt that the doctor on duty had not reported. She asked the nurse if she can serve the coffee to her father. It was okayed; she then headed for the ward. Masood was awake. His face bandage removed, and she could see the face. The grief and anxiety were visible on his face. On seeing Sharifa, he tried to shake his face. The cup of coffee brought life in him. Masood called Iqbal near, and looked at Abdullah to convey his greetings. Masood wanted to say something to Abdullah but controlled himself.

Sharifa told him that it may take a week more. One more week in the hospital and he will recover. Masood was just listening to Sharifa and conveyed his acceptance through his eyes.

As there was nothing much for him to do in hospital, Abdullah wanted to go back. Sharifa told him to go, and she will spend more time in the hospital with father. Abdullah went away.

CHAPTER 12

Masood was released from the hospital and came back home feeling tired but managed to walk.

- What you wish to eat? Let me know and will cook your preferred meal. You must be fed up eating the hospital food, Sharifa asked.
- No dear, I don't enjoy eating any more. Cook whatever you wish. Where is Iqbal?
- Oh! Iqbal is at Nisreen's house. Zeenat is there, and play together. I will call later in the evening. I will prepare Masoor Dal and Bhendi which you liked most. I am not as good a cook as mother.

Sharifa regretted having said that and changed the discussion at once.

- Abdullah had to go. The work is demanding, and now a day business is not doing well. The brothers in the family are fighting, and affecting business.
- What is the problem?
- Usual family issues. Money is the root of evil. We are happy with small family.
- Please open the cupboard of Maimuna?
- Yes, but now why?
- I want to show something and discuss the same.
- We can do later if you wish.
- How long you will be staying here. Abdullah is alone, and you too.
- Yes, but you need me too. Abdullah will manage.

There was a knock at the door. Sharifa went to open the door and saw uncle Hussain. She welcomed and asked if she can get a cup of coffee.

Hussain said no, but Sharifa insisted as she was going to get one for Masood, he can give company. Hussain agreed as he knew that she made an excellent coffee. Sharifa went to the kitchen, and Hussain went into see Masood.

- How are you now, he asked.
- Good by the grace of Allah. There is no pain, but movements are bit restricted.
- It will be fine soon, and you will be as active as ever.
- My life cannot be the same now. She has left, and I have now only memories. Allah had given an exceptionally dutiful wife.
- Pray for her—a choked Hussain could utter only these words.
- We are grateful to Allah for you and maybe HIS wish that you do something for her now so that her memories are cherished by everyone.
- What can I do?
- Yes, I have come to discuss the same with you.

Sharifa came with three cups of coffee.

Hussain asked her to sit and drink coffee. There is something to discuss with Masood.

- I have come to take you home. You will now stay with us, he said.
- Oh no, how that is possible? Masood objected.
- Don't worry everything is possible. Sharifa cannot stay here for long. She has the house to look after and Iqbal is missing school, and that is not acceptable.
- I don't need to be a burden on you.
- You are not a burden—you are the source through which I will see Allah's blessings. There is no argument or discussion on this issue. Once you are 100% well then you can choose.
- What do you think, Sharifa? He asked . . .
- Uncle, I can stay and look after, but Iqbal's missing school is problem too.
- So final now, no more discussion. You are coming home.
- Fine then, Maimuna has even taken care of me after leaving, he sighed with a relief.
- Now I have thought of doing something for my sister, and have come to discuss the same too.
- Yes, you were mentioning it to me. What is it?

- I want to start a scholarship in her name and give to the deserving student for further study.
- It is a brilliant idea, Sharifa intervened.
- The scholarship will be named after her. Will be called "Maimuna Memories", and will be awarded to the best student, who finishes first in the school. The boy can pursue the career of his choice—be a doctor, be a lawyer, be an engineer.

Be an Engineer? Sharifa dreamt of Iqbal. Is this a silent and blessed message from Allah!

- This is a noble idea. We will need a large fund. I honestly don't have an idea of the fund.
- I have checked with friends in the Trust which is for the school children. The Trust stops giving grant after school. Trust has no more funds and indicated that a fund Rs. 5 lacks is needed to start.
- It is an enormous sum. How to manage?
- Yes, I know, but Maimuna will find a way. Hussain folded the hands as offered in prayers. I am sure we can arrange. She is your wife and your consent and support are a must.
- I am for it. Let me get well soon, and we will review how to take it further. I am grateful to you for thinking so much for Maimuna— She was indeed a devoted wife to me.

The tears and chocked voice made the room atmosphere quiet. Hussain and Sharifa were in tears. Few moments passed in silence.

- I will now go to the office. Pack the essential things. I will come in the evening to take you home.
- No, wait for a day or two.
- Don't delay Sharifa for too many days, Iqbal is missing school.
- No, I will shift on Friday.
- Ok, then I go.

Hussain left.

CHAPTER 13

Masood called Sharifa and hugged her. Sharifa was in the arms of Masood. The father and daughter engrossed in tears. Spiritually both saw the face of Maimuna before their eyes.

- As you are now going, please open the cupboard. I want to discuss Maimuna's clothes and jewelleries.

Now this had to be done.

- You keep whatever clothes you need, and the rest can be distributed. You take the jewelleries and I don't have to worry. As we were going for marriage, she must have carried few jewellery which is now lost.
- I think we should give this to Uncle Hussain and let him decide.
- I also thought, but wanted to ask you first. There is jewellery which she had kept for Iqbal's bride. I have to fulfil her wish.

Iqbal's bride?—How concerned mother was? How much she had planned? Why has Allah taken her so early? Maybe HE needed her more than me. The thoughts flowing and she was lost.

- What are you thinking? Please open the drawer, we don't have much time.

She opened the cupboard and removed the case. The case had a diamond necklace. She was stunned at the sight of the necklace. She showed to Masood and again the memories of Maimuna flowed. Masood wanted Sharifa to take the necklace, but she convinced him that it was not safe in her house, and the necklace can stay with him. When Iqbal is married, he should offer himself to Iqbal's bride.

- I hope I am able to see that day, he said.
- Look at the dresses. See if you want to wear something, he continued.

Sharifa looked at the clothes, and saw Maimuna's wedding dress. She thought of Iqbal's bride and decided to keep the same dress for her.

- Check her savings box. She always used to save money and keep it aside. She had told me about the habit but not the details. How much is in the box? I certainly don't know.
- Sharifa removed the case. The case was bit heavy with a lock. They looked for the key but could not find and decided to break open.

When, opened there was a pile of 100 rupee notes. On counting, it totalled as 78600. This surprised Sharifa and Masood, not at the amount but at the number of 786 which was a religious significance for Allah. They decided that this will be given to Hussain Uncle for the Trust "Maimuna's Memories".

There was other purse where she used to keep her daily expense cash. She opened it and to her surprise the total was 2786. Masood asked her to keep this for herself, and she agreed. The Rs. 2000/—debt of Zaheda was on the back of her mind.

The hidden voice in Sharifa was knocking at her mind.

Sharifa asked mother's date of birth. She calculated the days. Maimuna had lived 17786 days to be precise. Again the "786" found in it.

She was curious, and asked Maimuna's wedding date. She was 6786 days old when married. Again the "786" was present.

On her birth—She calculated, and it was 7786 day of her life when Maimuna had become a mother. Again the "786" was found in it.

They both were shocked at this amazing aspect of Maimuna's life, and decided to keep this to themselves and not discuss with the family. Sharifa had decided to tell Iqbal at the proper time.

Beyond compassion!

Beyond confrontation!

Beyond comprehension!

On Friday Hussain came. They gave him the Savings box, the jewelleries and clothes to do the needful. Hussain accepted this as a donation from the deceased sister. They told him about the diamond necklace kept for Iqbal's bride and the wedding dress of Maimuna. Masood gave Sharifa a package and told her to be careful and open the same on reaching home. There was silence and nothing remained to be discussed.

Hussain dropped Sharifa and Iqbal to the bus stop and after bidding farewell Masood went to Husain's house.

CHAPTER 14

$\mathbf{O}$n reaching home, Sharifa had to do cleaning work. House was in shambles. Iqbal tried to help with whatever little help he could give. Shabana had gone away to play with the friends.

She opened the packet Masood had given to her. There were ten thousand rupees and a note which said, "Use this for the Fateha of Maimuna on the 40th day of death".

She went to Zaheda's house and see if she still needed her for the domestic work. Zaheda had recovered now, and said it was now not necessary and thanked Sharifa for taking care of her in illness, Zaheda offered her condolences on mother's death. Sharifa gave Rs. 2000 back to her and thanked for the help.

The loss of work was a concern for Sharifa, but had faith in Allah. Zaheda realised the stress on Sharifa's face and wanted to help her.

Abdullah came in the evening, and Sharifa told him. She has lost the job, but was glad that she repaid the debt.

- Did you pay money to her? What was the rush? You don't know how much debt I have on my head. If you had not paid her, she might have made you work and recovered her money. You are an idiot and don't know the life.
- It was a debt and father had given me the money to pay.
- Oh so now your father knows! He must have given you lot of money and jewelleries too.

Sharifa wanted to mention the sum of Rs. 10000/but her inner voice did not allow it.

41

She spoke of Hussain Uncle's idea of setting up a fund for higher studies in the name of her mother. Her jewelleries and money donated to the trust. She did not mention the Diamond Necklace for Iqbal's bride.

- You are generous donors and want to show your mighty name to the society. You don't care for the needs of your families and want to do something for others, he taunted.
- It was Uncle Husain's idea. May be Iqbal will be able to use that trust for his higher education. I want him to be an Engineer.
- Engineer? He said sarcastically. I will wait till he finishes school, and I have talked to my boss, and he will give Iqbal a job in the shop. I now cannot do everything. He has to help me. He is my son, and I will make him do what I want to do. I did what my father had asked me to do.
- No, I will not let it happen. Iqbal will study and be an engineer.
- I will see, he said.

Tabassum walked in and informed Sharifa that mom wanted to see her.

- Where is Iqbal, She inquired.
- He has gone to get the milk, Sharifa said.
- Is it urgent? Please tell Zaheda, I will come as soon as I have finished cooking.
- I don't know, I will tell her. You please bring Iqbal with you. I have new toys and want to play with him.

She had a big sneeze and wiped her running nose with her frock.

- Now that is not decent, where is the handkerchief, Sharifa said.
- Oh I always use my dress. My mom never tells me anything.
- That is because she loves you and does not need to annoy you.
- So you don't love me, she said mischievously.
- I do love you, but I want you to be decent.
- What does Iqbal do when he has a stuffy nose?
- He uses a handkerchief, of course.
- So next time I will give him my frock, come soon and bring Iqbal with you, she laughed and ran away.

Sharifa laughed at childhood's simplicity and reflected back on her childhood. She was the same.

Sharifa came to meet Zaheda. Iqbal was with her. Tabassum came running and caught hold of Iqbal and took him to her room.

- I have found this work for you. If you want to have.
- Yes, indeed, I want it.

- It is bit far away; will you be able to manage?
- How far?
- It is at my aunt's house, say 30 minutes from here.
- What is the work?
- Usual cooking and cleaning and they will pay you decent salary too.
- How much?
- I think Rs.1500 per month. I will talk to them and see if they can give more.
- See if you can, as I have to be away from the house for a longer time. I have to worry about Iqbal and Shabana too.
- That is what I thought, but decided to check with you. They are decent people and will take care of you well.
- I will let you know after I talk to Abdullah.

She called for Iqbal.

- Aunty let him play here, please.
- No, he has to do his studies also.
- Why he has to study always let him play too, we have not finished our game yet.
- Ok fine. Finish it and come back soon.
- Thank you so much. I promise. I will not give him my frock when he sneezes.

She took hold of Iqbal and ran away.

- What is she saying? Zaheda didn't understand
- Oh nothing, you know how lively and innocent she is? She was just teasing me.

On reaching home Sharifa told Abdullah about the new job offered by Zaheda. The pay was reasonable, but the problem is where to keep the children when they return from school as she will not be home at that time.

- What is the pay?
- Rs. 1500
- That is good; it will be of much help to me.
- But what about children?
- Oh don't worry about them; they will play here and there. It is a matter of 2-3 hours.
- No, it may spoil them. Iqbal has to finish the homework too.
- You think of Iqbal and nothing but Iqbal.
- I have to think about him.

- Then you think but don't let that job go away. I want that income. I have to go to work now.

Abdullah went away. Shabana was thinking. Can she ask Zaheda to take care of the children till she returns? Who else will help her? She had to do something.

She made up her mind and went to Zaheda.

- I discussed with Abdullah, and he agreed.
- That is good. Can you then start from tomorrow?
- There is a problem of looking after children when they come back from school. I came to ask your help if you can look after them for that much time.
- Cannot tell you now. Let me speak to Hamid and see what he says.
- Yes, you must ask him, but he will be in office and will have no distraction from them.
- I am sure of Iqbal but not sure of Shabana. She will pick up fight with Tabassum, and I will have a hard time. She won't listen to me.
- You don't worry about it, I will tell Shabana, and she will behave.
- I will help you for few days. If they behave well, then nothing to worry . . .
- That is so nice of you. Allah will bless you. I will then start the work from tomorrow.

Sharifa left with anxious thoughts about Shabana.

Will she cause any problem?

CHAPTER 15

Masood recovered well with the attention from the family of Hussain, and wanted to go back home.

- I have now recovered and can look after, please let me go. I have to start the work and look after the school.
- Why you have to go and work for the school. I think you retire now.
- No, retirement for me. I have a long way to go.
- Can I ask you something?
- Yes, please don't hesitate.
- You are now alone. Who takes care of the house and the daily kitchen issues?
- No, I am not alone, Maimuna is with me still, and I can handle the kitchen. I don't want sumptuous food now. I am sure I can handle.
- No, I was thinking why you don't you re-marry and continue with your life. I am sure Maimuna in Jannat will be happy with it.
- What are you saying Hussain? A shocked Masood shouted.
- I am not telling you now. We wait for some time and give a thought. There is nothing wrong. Allah has permitted the re-marriage. One has to move on with life.
- No, I will not do it. Please don't raise this issue any time. I will meet Maimuna in Jannat when my time comes. That will be the only re-marriage, I will endure in my afterlife.
- I respect your thoughts, but I wanted to be practical. There is nothing wrong in it. Allah will be most pleased, if you marry a widow and take care of her.
- No, I will not think about it.

- The issue of the Trust which we decided to start is to be looked into . . . If you can now give your time, and see how we can start. You are experienced in the Trust matters.
- Yes, indeed that is the priority in life. I will pick up the issue with the authorities. But first I have to find out how much fund is required in a year for the Trust.
- They told me an estimate of Rs. 5 lacs to start.
- I have to discuss with them and work out perfect strategy. I think 5 lacs will be a much higher amount. But whatever, I am committed to your noble idea, and will give my best effort. I am sure Allah is with me. Then I will leave this Friday after the prayers. Is it ok with you?
- As you wish, but you can stay here as long as you wish. I think re-marriage is a good option and there is nothing wrong. You know Shirin, must be the same age of Maimuna. She became widow last year, and if I suggest she may consider the proposal. Her late husband worked in Gulf. She can be an enjoyable life-partner too.
- No, I don't like her life to be spoiled. I am sure she will find someone else. I have closed this chapter, and I will not re-open it. Please understand my feelings too. I beg you.
- I am sorry; we will end this chapter here. So Friday, you want to leave.
- Yes, Inshallah.

On Friday after prayers Masood went to his house.

He sat on the rocking chair. This was the first time he was alone after the death of Maimuna. There was no Sharifa, no Iqbal, and no Hussain. His eyes became wet. He wanted to cry, but tears did not come out. He felt the life had become stale now. With his closed eyes, he could roll back the happy occasions of life with Maimuna.

He was rocking, and the events were just rolling before the eyes. On the first meeting how nervous and shivering she was. She avoided looking at him straight in the face. She wore a simple but colourful kurta/shalwar a combination of purple and green colour. His most favourites—was it a coincidence or a message from Almighty that she is destined to be your wife and to accept her.

The marriage was a simple event in the family as both the parents believed in simplicity. The Nikah performed in the mosque, and they became husband and wife.

They were happy—it was a joint family and had restrictions of joint family on their freedom of married life. He recollected how she avoided coming before him when he was with his father.—He laughed at those subtle days of his life. Now the times have changed.

Allah blessed them with a daughter, and that day was the happiest day of their life. They were alone in the hospital, and he had held the hands of Maimuna-looked at her and out of impulse had kissed her. This was the first time it was outside the bedroom. He trembled at his behaviour in the public place like this—he was laughing and enjoying the recollections.

Sharifa's birth was a happy event for the family. A child born after 18 years, and Sharifa was the main source of love, laughs and laziness.

Maimuna was again pregnant after three years but had a difficult time. Her health was taking a toll and the doctors advised her complete rest. She was not to get involved in any domestic work. This was a difficult time but had brought Sharifa more near to him. She had just started talking, and with her innocent words and gestures provided the relief to him in those difficult days.

It was a pre-matured birth and doctors told that Maimuna had suffered a serious injury and cannot conceive again, and he should take care. This was a shock to him, at this young stage of their life. But he had immense faith in Allah and Sharifa was there.

He went to sleep on the chair, Maimuna was in the dreams. Her face was now more radiant. There was radiance everywhere in the room. She was at peace with her eternal life. Maimuna looked at him. Masood sensed as if she pleaded something, he woke and got up from the chair. Masood felt as if she held his hand, and took him somewhere. She took him to their bedroom and showed him the empty bed.

He heard a voice—I have played my role, which Allah had destined for me. I have given you a child by his blessings, and we both gave her the best things in life. She is now blessed with our grandson, and our duty to take care of him. Sharifa's life is not as happy as ours, but she is not complaining. Take care of both now, and you alone cannot do it—listen to what Hussain is saying to you. You have the permission from me, and the blessings of Allah— The voice disappeared. There was silence and the divine light disappeared.

It was quiet, and he was wide awake. He was trembling from the message he received. Was it proper?—But how can he do justice to re-marriage? Is Shirin the right woman? No doubt she is rich. Will she be a trustworthy partner for him? He decided to share his dream with Hussain and then settle the matter.

Masood felt he had no choice.

Masood felt he had no options.

CHAPTER 16

Sharifa's new domestic work was more time consuming. She felt that attention to Iqbal was getting less and less, and this may take away attention from studies. Iqbal was getting more playful because of time with Tabassum and this may become harmful.

Sharifa once talked to Zaheda

- How did the children behaved? I hope I am not troubling you too much.
- No, they are playing and not fighting. Shabana is not mixing, but is Ok. She is not creating much trouble and goes out and plays with friends.
- The people at work are extremely polite, and understand my difficulties and always let me to leave on time without bothering too much. I am truly grateful for this job.
- I am glad that I could do something. On the contrary, Tabassum has now become serious in school work which she was not bothered earlier. I have had to spend so much time with her, and Iqbal takes care of that. She does home work and takes Iqbal's help whenever required. And does not trouble. I think you have to talk to Shabana. She has to be more attentive and careful. She is now becoming a teenager from a child, and she has to be informed and advised of her age issues . . . Unfortunately, she has no mother, and we have to do it. She does not listen and is not willing to spend time with me. You must do it. She is now your responsibility.
- Yes, indeed, she is my responsibility and I will do it. Give my salams to Hamidbhai and I will leave now.

On reaching home, Sharifa discussed the issue of Shabana with Abdullah.

- She is now maturing and has to know the responsibilities in life.
- It is your responsibility, how can I discuss these issues.
- I know, but she will not talk to me. I was thinking to get help from someone with whom she is friendlier. You can tell me if you know someone.
- No, I don't know anybody. This woman's issue is to be handled by you only. How can I talk to someone?
- Well then I have thought of someone—her school teacher. I will meet, and she should be able to help.
- See, you are unnecessarily worried and make life so complicated. We don't have to worry. They learn by themselves.
- It is not that easy. Right guidance at the right time is extremely essential for the girl. Now life is so much open and vulnerable that a girl can be misled and life ruined.

She decided to visit school and get the help of teacher.

CHAPTER 17

Hussain came to visit Masood and wanted to discuss the Trust. He had spoken to few friends and got financial commitments from few who liked the concept.

Hussain said to Masood,

- I spoke to few friends supporting the Trust. Many are even willing to give donation.
- I am not yet able to talk to anybody. I have still not come out of the grief of death, Masood replied.
- I understand feelings but be at ease. My idea was to announce the launch of Charity Trust on anniversary day, now few days away. What do you say?
- I want to be sure of the same before the announcement and be sure that it is possible to execute the plan. I don't wish to let her suffer in divine state of life. It has to be done, but be sure.
- I agree, and convinced that it will happen. We have the blessings of Allah. I spoke to Shirin. She is willing to support.
- What! You spoke to Shirin. How can you do that?
- I spoke of the idea of the Charitable Trust and charity.
- Are you telling the truth? You don't see through what turmoil I am passing these days. Maimuna comes in dreams and asking to follow your suggestion of re-marriage. I have sleepless nights.
- I am telling the truth. The issue of re-marriage was not discussed. I discussed the charity part and the idea of the trust. Shirin's memories of Maimuna are blurred as after marriage she was in Gulf for so long and cannot re-collect. Now what you are telling me is that

re-marriage is Maimuna's wish. I should take up the issue. I will need help from Ali and Nisreen.

- You will not take any action without my consent. I have to talk to Sharifa and get her approval too.
- If you say so, I will talk to Sharifa on your behalf. It will be better that I talk. Any how I am going to Mumbai day after to-morrow for the trust work; I will meet Sharifa and seek approval too.
- No, No, No—I talk to my daughter.
- How can you talk to your daughter on your re-marriage? I think she will be embarrassed, and you may lose your self-respect. I will suggest to her as my idea and seek her approval. Any how it was my idea and I thought and created this situation for you.
- What about Shirin?—She has to decide first to it. Her family has to accept the idea too.
- Yes, indeed—I never thought. The relatives are independent and settled in their lives. I don't think they will mind her re-marriage. This thought never occurred to me. How come it came to you? He teased Masood.
- Yes, I understand the taunt, but getting tormented by this idea of re-marriage. I am tormented by Maimuna's appeals to me in the dreams. I think on the pros and cons of this idea. You have had mentioned her wealth. Wealth is always an issue which needs to be resolved, and that is how I was thinking who else in her family is interested in wealth. I had to find out, and know the family. I don't know them, but that could be an issue. I am not interested in the wealth. I don't need, and don't want any complications in life at this stage.
- I am sorry if I have hurt your feelings, but you are right as always. My respect goes much deeper. I will try to find out this. Give a day or two. As the idea of re-marriage is acceptable, speaking to Sharifa is my responsibility.
- Yes, find out the details first. Talk to Shirin and see what she has to say. Please don't give name or involve me. Shirin has to accept the thought of re-marriage and know what the expectations are. If everything is ok, then I prefer to talk to her first.
- Yes, I agree with the idea, and I will involve Nisreen in this to take up the matter further. I will propose as an idea, and meet Shirin and understand her opinion on re-marriage.

Hussain left, leaving Masood alone.

While sitting on chair, he saw the face of Maimuna. She was smiling and was looking with contended eyes. Masood could not resist this; he closed the eyes and wanted to be near to Maimuna.

CHAPTER 18

As discussed with Masood, Hussain decided to meet Nisreen and seek help to get view point of Shirin.

Nisreen, I have come to seek your help, Hussain Said.

My help? Let me know how can I help?

- I have been thinking of remarriage of Masood. He is alone and I am sure this loneliness will be difficult for him to endure for long. He has to get involved in an active life again.
- I agree with you, but think to be a difficult decision for him. As far as I know they both were perfect partners and dedicated to each other. I am sure Masoodbhai will not agree to it. Have you asked him?
- Yes I have asked, but he is not ready for it. I had a long discussion. Masood listened, but not objected. I have a lady in my mind, and I need your help in talking to her and get her opinion and consent.
- Who is she? Do you have someone in mind?
- Yes I have, but I cannot talk to her and for this reason, I have come to you and need your help. The matter has to be between two of us and nobody should know. Masood's name should not be taken unless the lady has given her consent. Can you do this?—Allah will bless you.
- I understand, please let me know who she is.
- It is Shirin
- Which Shirin? Are you talking of the widow of Rahimbhai, who expired last year?

- Yes you are right; I am talking of the same lady. She is a widow and must be of same age of Maimuna. She is religious and could be an ideal partner for Masood

- But she is rich and had a fabulous and abundant life in Gulf. I don't think she will now opt for this difficult life. I heard that she plans to go back to the gulf.

- I am not aware of this. What will she do there? There is nothing wrong to meet her and seek her viewpoint.

- I will try, but I don't know her well to discuss this issue with her. Can I get help of someone who knows her?

- Now the more you talk to people, the word spreads, and not proper for both of them. People always try to dig up the issues. I suggest you meet her, get intimacy and closeness and then raise the issue later. I suggest, invite her for a lunch . . .

- For lunch without any reason, I will have to ask Ali.

- I have a valid reason and no one will even say no to it. Next Friday is Prophet's Birthday. You can organise a woman's Majalis on that day and invite few friends. Invite Shirin too. Tell Ali that you wanted to do this Majalis since long, and I am sure he will not object to it. It will involve expense which I will take care of it. I will get blessings of Allah.

- Yes a brilliant idea, I will talk to Ali take approval and organise the Majalis.

Hussain left with the pleasure of having achieved something and prayed that Nisreen will be able to do the work.

There was no question by Ali when Nisreen asked. Nisreen organised the same on the Friday.

The Majalis finished in time, and when people were leaving, Nisreen asked Shirin and Sarah to stay for more time as she needed help. Sarah and Shirin were intimate friends, and Nisreen wanted to get closer to Shirin with the help of Sarah.

- It was gracious of you to come at short notice, Nisreen said.

- How one can deny the invitation for Prophet's Majalis, Shirin replied.

- This was my long cherished wish, which Allah fulfilled today. You must be having Majalis in Dubai.

- Yes we do have, but Majalis in India is different. It is simple and invokes religious feelings in you.

- Dubai must be fascinating, we have heard so much. Dubai is expensive but the life is easy. I wish I can go there once to see it.
- Well life is not easy for everyone. By the grace of Allah, Rahim had a good job, and we had a decent life. I have photos of our life in Dubai—Why don't you come to my house for a cup of tea. You can see our Album and get an idea of Dubai. May be Allah will fulfil your dream and you can go to Dubai to see it, one day.

It was an excellent opportunity, and Nisreen never wanted to miss it.

- I will be most happy and will make it one of these days. I will note your phone number and will talk to you later.

They exchanged the phone numbers. After good gossips, they asked for permission to go, Nisreen offered tea as it was tea-time and insisted on it.

After tea, they departed.

She is friendly and talkative, Shirin said to Sarah.

Yes, talkative and can be a good company to you, Sarah said.

The days passed, and Nisreen took the opportunity to develop closeness by calling at least once a day. She delayed her visit to Shirin's house as she wanted to develop an intimate relationship to raise the issue of re-marriage.

After a month, she planned visit to her house.

It was a well furnished house, but simplicity was there. There was no show of wealth. She liked it and praised her for a magnificent house. She viewed the Album of Shirin—saw lovely photos of her past and was bit confused and puzzled on the thought of re-marriage.

Time passed, she and Shirin became closer and closer. This closeness brought the dark side of her married life. She realised that Rahim was not a loving husband. He had his own style of life, and the conflict was always a strain in their life. Shirin had to go through many dark days and as she was in Dubai far away from the family, had no choice but to accept it as a fate of life and never complained.

- I honestly regret your married life,—Nisreen said
- Yes, but what could I have done as a woman, I got used to it and started accepting it. I used to ask always, Allah to forgive me and get me the love of a husband which a woman wants. The days passed. Rahim's health deteriorated because of the habits and one day Allah took him away. I accepted it as my fate and devoted my life now to more simplicity and in spirituality.
- But you are still in mid-age. You can think of re-marriage.

- Remarriage? What are you talking? My married life was so hard that I can never think of another man in my life. I am happy as I am.
- You are right and equally wrong too. Allah wants a woman to have a husband—a loving husband—a husband who can take care—a husband for whom you pray. You had a difficult marriage, but you never know the ways of Allah.
- Yes, indeed Allah's ways are unknown to us. We have to accept and live with what HE blesses us. I do that. Rahim has left enough, but have to take care of it, else it will be over and then the life will be difficult.
- Yes, the costs are increasing every day. If you don't manage funds to meet the increased costs, then it will wipe out soon. You are blessed with funds, why don't you invest in business so that you earn a living from it?
- I don't know anything about business, and cannot trust anyone with the money. Things are hard now days.
- It is true. We have compassionate people in our village that will take care of your funds and give you a decent income so that you can live in comfort.
- Should I talk to Ali and see if he has any suggestion?

Nisreen mentioned Ali, but behind her mind it was always Masood, but she was cautious and never wanted to mention Masood now.

- I am not sure. And it will involve unnecessary complications in my life. I think I will manage myself.
- Yes that is the way Allah has taken care of you. Yet a loving husband is needed in life. I think Allah has given that task to me. I will have to find a suitable husband for you.

They both laughed.

Nisreen met Hussain to keep him informed. Shirin's difficult married life and the dilemma of source of income.

Hussain saw this as the right opportunity. He asked Nisreen to give the example of Prophet and Khadija. Khadija was a wealthy widow who trusted Prophet with the business and married him. He was sure that if Masood is introduced with this concept and faith, the things may work better.

He imposed this thought into the mind of Nisreen, which thrilled her at the similarity. She got motivated and excited to play her role with commitment.

She met Shirin and said,

- Look I have found an honest person who will take care of your wealth. He is honest and has an excellent reputation in the society.
- Who is he? I have not heard of this person.
- No you might not have, because he is a simple man. Let me give you an example. She then narrated the life story of Prophet to her as advised by Hussain.
- Shirin shocked at the similarity and laughed.
- These men do not exist anymore, she said sarcastically. It is a sin to compare someone to be Prophet. Allah may not forgive you.
- I am not comparing him with Prophet. I just gave you an example of what Allah did for Khadija. It will be a sin to compare someone with Prophet, and my Allah knows I never meant it that way.
- I am sorry if I hurt your feelings. Please forgive me.

Nisreen lost her strength and could not try further, felt guilty of having listened to Hussainbhai. The concept of Prophet should not have been involved in these worldly affairs.

Nisreen took leave of Shirin and went away.

The whole conversation left a deep impact on Shirin.

Shirin was thinking who is that man about whom Nisreen is talking is. She was eager to find out and was considering trusting him with funds and creating a credible source of income out of it. The funds may last not more than five years, and after that life could be depressed. The thought of that life shocked her. She searched for the solution and prayed to Allah.

The thought of re-marriage entered in her mind.

But she did not know what to do. She wondered. Is Nisreen a help sent by Allah?

The thought confused her.

The thought also excited her.

CHAPTER 19

Maimuna's death anniversary arrived, and Masood wanted to do it with the religious piety.

He had to depend on Hussain, Ali and Nisreen to organise the same. He wanted Sharifa to come and be a part of the same. When the news came that Sharifa will be coming with Iqbal, he was most happy.

Hussain and Nisreen wanted to take this opportunity of introducing Shirin to Sharifa and Masood.

Sharifa arrived, and Nisreen to took her away.

- Masoodbhai is alone, and what do you think of the remarriage, she asked Sharifa.
- I don't know whether he will agree to it.

She was puzzled with this idea but composed while replying.

- Hussainbhai has talked to him and now he needs your help to convince him. We know he is alone and needs a company to live. Allah has not objected to re-marriage and on the contrary Quran advises the re-marriage of widows.
- Is someone in your mind which my father will accept?
- Yes, I want you to meet her first, and see if you approve her.
- Who is she, when and where I can see her? Does she know my father?
- No, she does not know him. I invited her for the Majalis and will introduce. She was in Dubai and became a widow year ago. She is rich.
- My father needs a simple and pious woman in his life.

- She must be of the same age of Maimuna and is trustworthy and pious. You meet her, and then we will see.
- I will be happy to meet her and hope can help my father to spend his remaining life under proper care.

Next day, Sharifa met Shirin. The introduction was not difficult as it was her mother's death. Shirin expressed her condolences, and prayed for Maimuna.

Shirin inquired about Sharifa's life. Sharifa gave her a brief detail and mentioned Iqbal. Shirin invited Sharifa to visit her, but Sharifa could not accept it and told that she will be leaving tomorrow as Iqbal cannot miss the school. Abdullah is alone and cannot manage the house. He could not come because of the work in the shop and the young sister-in-law needs attention. Shirin had good impression of Sharifa and her manners of talking and respect she was giving to her.

- She is impressive and dignified, she said to Nisreen. It is a pity that Sharifa lost mother at this age when she needed her most. But one never knows the ways of Allah.
- Yes, she is talented and understanding—she got the best training and guidance from father since childhood and mother who was equally religious.
- It is gratifying to understand the role of father in one's life. That gives the children the knowledge of real world and makes them more competitive in the world. She is lucky to have a father who cares so much. Who is he?
- Would you meet him? Nisreen was happy and shocked to hear this question by her.

Shirin felt embarrassed by the question. She was reflecting on her childhood and the treatment she got from her father.

- No, no it just came out of curiosity. It is not proper for me to meet him. I prefer to go now.

On the way, she saw Sharifa talking with someone whom she presumed must be her father.

She had a look at him and impressed by his posture and dignified look.

On reaching home, she thought, Nisreen was talking about the father of Sharifa. The man had no doubt impressed her, and wanted to find out more. She had seen the daughter and made the first assessment of him.

After people had left, Masood was with Sharifa alone.

- Your life must be lonely and hard now, Sharifa said.

- No, I have memories to live with, and I am happy.
- Why don't you think of re-marriage?
- What are you talking? I am sure Hussain must have passed this thought to you.
- Yes, he has but what is wrong with it. I am sure my mother will be most pleased in heaven. Nisreen Aunty has introduced me to her and I love her. She will be a loving wife to you and a loving mother.
- Did you meet her? When and where?
- In the Majalis, she was there. Her name is Shirin. She is a widow and intends to re-marry.
- How do you know?
- I did meet her but not spoken re-marriage as it was not the right occasion. Nisreen Aunty wants to take the matter further, needed my help to get your consent. I will be most pleased if you agree to it.
- I cannot tell you now—but meet her and talk to her.
- I will ask Nisreen Aunty, and it can be arranged. But I am leaving tomorrow as cannot stay for long.
- Better you stay and have a meeting with her
- I love to, but you understand how Abdul is?—Shabana is alone, and Iqbal will miss the school.
- Ok as you please, I am doing this because you want me to do it.

Sharifa conveyed to Nisreen the reluctant consent of her father and prayed well for him.

Nisreen conveyed this message to Hussain at once, and now they had to convey it to Shirin and organise the meeting.

CHAPTER 20

After a week, Nisreen invited them for dinner to her house. Hussain, Ali, and Sarah were present.

- This is Masoodbhai, whose daughter you met at the Majalis, Nisreen introduced Masood to Shirin.
- They exchanged traditional greetings and she took seat next to Sarah, holding Sarah's hand. Sarah felt the nervousness in her hand and hold it to give the moral support.

After serving the welcome drinks and snacks, Nisreen started the topic.

- Masoodbhai lost his wife in a tragic car accident a year ago. You met his daughter Sharifa in the Majalis. She is the only daughter. Her mother Maimuna was a noble woman and a devoted wife. We loved her, but Allah loved her most and HE called her back to HIM.

She continued, now addressing to Masood.

- Masoodbhai she is Shirin. She lost her husband last year. They were in Dubai, and she returned back after his death. You must know her father, Ijjajbhai who was working here with the municipal office. Hussainbhai knew him. Shirin is now alone—no children and I am asking her to re-marry.
- I have forced her to meet you today and then take a decision. Hussainbhai has supported me in my choice. Now two of you meet and understand each other.

Masood did not answer but looked at Shirin—but she was quiet and not looking at him.

Hussain said, Masood, you two talk and consider it out.

- Yes, true, I and Sarah will go to the kitchen and start preparation for lunch. Hussainbhai and Ali can go to market and bring the sweets, which I ordered.
- Sure, Ali got up and asked Hussain to come with him, and they left. Nisreen and Sarah went to the kitchen and had a mischievous look at Shirin.
- I am forced by Hussain and my daughter for this re-marriage, Masood had to start the conversation. Maimuna was a devoted wife, and we have had a happy married life. Her passing created a void in my life. I am a simple man with simple life. I am not rich, but I earn enough to take care of family. Sharifa and grandson Iqbal are strengths of life. I cannot promise you the luxuries of life which you must have had in your Gulf life. Please tell me something. There is no pressure if you don't want. If you have any question, I answer.

Shirin was quiet and nervous.

- I have nothing to ask, she spoke softly.

The sweetness and clarity of her voice shook Masood as it was so similar to that of Maimuna.

- If you have any questions, please convey me through Nisreen, and I will clarify it. Or if you want my number I will give it to you and you can talk to me.
- Yes, please give me your number.

Masood gave the number, which she wrote in her diary. This was the opportunity for Masood to see her hand and was stunned by the femininity of it and the diamond ring in her hand. Her nails were so clean, shining and polished.

- I will go now and help Nisreen in the kitchen.

She looked at Masood for the first time. Their eyes faced each other, and she left the room.

In the kitchen, the two ladies looked at her. The freshness of her face convinced them that she had given her consent.

Hussain and Ali returned, and lunch was served. During lunch, Ali and Hussain discussed the development of Trust.

- It is going on but taking sometime. I have to get the necessary funds. The trustees are of the opinion that the trust corpus should be minimal 3-5 lacks and then the expenses of the college scholarship for higher education can be funded from the income of the corpus. I am talking to few good companies for charity, and I am sure something positive will come out of it. I have complete confidence that the Trust will be formed.

- Yes, indeed, a worthy cause and it will happen.
- Masoodbhai, what is your opinion on the changing social values in life?-, Nisreen asked.

Her main aim was to impress Shirin with the answer of Masood to show her, his knowledge and views on life.

- Yes, the values are changing but cannot disappear from one's life. It is the upbringing, intellectual development and retaining the core values. Unfortunately, the values, which, parents implanted in us, are not being transferred to our next generation. The expanse of knowledge is so rapid that the core knowledge is pushed back far deep into our mindset. We lost our access to it. It is here that the faith rooted in our life by the values taught to us by our parents can play a significant role to enlighten us. This is a complex and serious issue, we can talk at a proper time.

But let me tell you in a lighter vein, continued Masood,

Shaitan went to Allah and asked,

- Are you sure? You are not going to send another Prophet to the world?
- No, certainly not.
- You are not going to change your mind seeing the status of your creation.
- No, I have said that in Q'uran.

Shaitan laughed and said then I will send mine to the world.

Allah smiled. Shaitan then sent Internet.

- Now you see the havoc internet is playing in this world. With its goodness, being misused to create mistrust, exploit people and play with morality of the generation. It was true when Allah used to send the Prophet. The people who believed in him accepted his message and followed the right path. The one who did not, created the same chaos.

They laughed at the joke. Shirin was quiet and impressed by his way of talking and confidence in his faith.

Two days passed, and Masood received a call.

- I am Shirin and she exchanged the greetings.
- I am so happy that you called, I was waiting for it.

- I want to talk to you. The Trust discussed at Nisreen's House. I learnt more, and wish to give the funds to the Trust so that it can start at once. I have the savings which can be used for this charitable cause.
- But that is not correct, the funds you have is for your living and take care of you for the rest of your life. You can offer the excess funds.
- No, I have Allah to take care of me. I have you to take care of me.

Masood was stunned. What are you saying, he just could not continue?

- Allah has given the consent, and I accept the proposal. I will be now your responsibility.
- Can I now meet you to discuss it further?
- Yes, but I will not come alone, Nisreen will be with me.
- Why she?
- It will not be right for me to meet you alone. If you have any questions, call me.
- I respect your views.
- I will inform Nisreen. You have my answer. Do not tell that I spoke to you . . .

She closed the phone.

She informed Nisreen.

Shirin's consent, conveyed to Hussain. Everyone was happy and looked ahead to the Nikah Ceremony to be organised.

Sharifa was informed. She was happy on the decision of Masood and Shirin.

Hussain took the main task of organising the same.

Within a fortnight the day fixed, Sharifa—Iqbal and Abdullah arrived for the occasion. Hussain performed the role of Shirin's brother and a simple ritual of Nikah performed in the Mosque.

Hussain took this opportunity of announcing the formation of the Trust "Maimuna Memories" and the trust was now able to afford higher studies scholarship for the deserving students of schools. Sharifa thought that now her dream of making Iqbal an engineer will be fulfilled.

A simple routine traditional lunch was served.

At home, Sharifa was busy making Shirin familiar with the various complexities of the house. At tea time, she prepared the tea and served to them. Shirin was trying to get used to the new house. Ali, Nisreen and Sarah left after tea. Hussain and Masood were busy discussing the creation of Trust and how to complete the formalities.

After the dinner, Hussain left leaving the family alone.

Sharifa left with Iqbal and Abdullah, leaving Masood and Shirin alone in their room.

There was silence and both were just looking at each other. Finally, Masood had to start

- I am grateful to you for what you have done for the Trust and Allah will reward you for that.
- He has rewarded me and now you are in my life.

Masood got up and took hold of her hand. She responded to his holding by coming closer to with closed eyes.

A man and woman had turned into husband and wife.

Sharifa prepared the breakfast in the morning. She wanted to leave and go back. Shirin insisted for her to stay with them for few more days, but Iqbal's School and as she had left Shabana with Zaheda, she had to go. Abdullah had to go to work, and it was not possible to extend the stay.

They went leaving them alone. Her void was felt in the house. Masood was quiet and trying to get adjusted to the new woman in his life.

CHAPTER 21

After Hamid went to office, Tabassum put on the best dress and wanted to go and meet Iqbal. Hamid's offer of finding a respectable job for Iqbal had excited her.

Before leaving she asked mother. Zaheda looked with a smile and asked why so beautifully dressed?

- Where are you going in this beautiful dress at this time?
- Mom, going to Sharifa aunt's house to tell Iqbal that dad wants to meet in the evening.

But, why this beautiful dress?

Oh Mom you don't understand, you only told me that whenever you are going for pious work you must wear the best dress because an Angel will be walking with you. I am going to tell Iqbal that dad is going to get a decent job for him, and want Angel to be there at that time with me. With a mischievous smile, she looked at Zaheda.

Zaheda could not resist the argument and smiled.

Tabassum came to Iqbal's house and knocked the door.

Sharifa opened the door and surprised to see Tabassum at this time of the day in a lovely dress.

She welcomed Tabassum and asked the purpose of visit.

I came to tell Iqbal that dad wants to meet and he should come to house.

- Any reason? Sharifa asked.
- I honestly don't the reason. But where is Iqbal?

Iqbal has just gone to the market for shopping and should be back.

Ok then I go. Tell Iqbal to meet dad, preferably after Maghreb Prayers?

I will tell, but have a cup of tea or sherbet. I will get one for you.

No, aunty I will go—she was disappointed that Iqbal did not meet and started walking back.

On the way, she saw Iqbal coming to the house.

Tabassum's passion rushed back, and had that mischievous smile. She could not control and shouted.

Iqbal saw Tabassum and was anxious. She dressed so well and looking attractive.

Tabassum came running and held his hand.

- Iqbal, dad wants to meet you.
- Your dad but why?—What does he want? Have I done something wrong?

Iqbal could not control the nervousness.

- He is angry and has found out something, I don't know what.

Tabassum's mischievous nature took over, and wanted to tease

- Oh God, What can it be? Is it the book? What will he do?

Iqbal lost the strength and wanted to runaway, and never to meet Hamid

- But today I am going to Nana's house and will be away for few days—I can't meet today.

Tabassum knew it was a big lie else aunty Sharifa would have mentioned. She had taken control over Iqbal's fear and wanted to exploit it.

- What time will you be leaving?
- The bus leaves at 4 in the evening so I will leave around 2. Uncle comes from office at 6. It will not be possible to meet.
- Don't worry I will tell dad to come home early so that he can meet you.
- No, No don't do that. I will meet after I come back.

Having spoken now he regretted having uttered a lie.

Iqbal had forgotten the teaching of his mother. Never say lies and always tell truth. Her message that "Allah loves the truth and nothing but the truth"

Iqbal said, he was sorry and lied. He was not going anywhere but does not need to meet Hamid as he might have seen him with the book.

- I hope he has not seen us with the book. Else why he wants to meet me?

Tabassum had a worried look and the smile had gone.

This problem certainly gave a shock to Tabassum. Yes, indeed why? The father never bothered to inquire about Iqbal earlier.

The entire memory shot back in mind. On that evening when she was returning she had heard the father saying to mother, "Yes I have seen it".— These were the exact words.

Tabassum became confused and scared. Has father seen them together while returning from office, and they did not see him? She realised the condition of father that night after he had returned from the mosque. Did he visited the sweetmeat shop and found out something? She could not connect Hamid's sudden illness to the denial of Ashraf. She thought it cannot be because of that. What was it then? She realised that next day first time Hamid had inquired about Iqbal. Why?

Tabassum was nervous and held the hand of Iqbal more firmly.

Tensed Iqbal had forgotten the questions he had in mind which he was to ask Tabassum on the next meeting.

Iqbal saw fear in the eyes of Tabassum. He knew he had to take the control and find a solution. Tabassum tried to wipe the face with the shalwar—as her usual habit—Iqbal stopped her and offered the handkerchief—the dress was too beautiful to be spoiled.

He told Tabassum not to worry and if required will take the blame and will save her from any disgrace.

Iqbal told he will meet Hamid and see what the issue is. He wanted to put a brave face, but within was shivering.

Tabassum returned home. Her face pale and that smile had vanished.

- What happened? Why are you worried?
- Mom I am alright—I could not meet Iqbal, so I have left a message with Sharifa aunty.

She went in room and left Zaheda thinking.

CHAPTER 22

Shabana's arrogant behaviour increasing day by day, which Sharifa could not take it any longer. Regular late coming became a stress and concern for her and wanted to discuss the same with Abdullah.

One day Sharifa spoke to Abdullah.

- Talk to Shabana. She is coming home late and does not tell where she goes.
- So what? This is Mumbai, not the village! Shabana has friends, and has to go out, Abdullah retarded.
- Staying away for late nights is not advisable for young girl.
- Don't worry, Shabana is my sister.
- She is my sister too, and I am worried. I am worried for Hasmukh with whom she is so friendly.
- Who Hasmukh—Did I meet him? Why not tell earlier? You are an idiot.
- Yes, that is what I am trying to tell. Find a suitable boy and get her married.
- Get her married—now?"
- Yes, she is 21, and should be married now. I married at 18, and became a mother at 21.
- How can I? I have no money for marriage. Where will I get a boy?"
- That is our responsibility. Sell my jewelleries if you wish, but getting her married is our primary duty. Allah has given this responsibility and need to finish it.

Abdullah cooled down—Sharifa's offer of her jewellery gave relief.

Abdullah said, he will talk to Shabana, and speak to Shahid's mother to look for the boy.

After Sharifa's information, Abdullah wanted to speak with Shabana of marriage but was not finding the right occasion for it.

Abdullah had no suitable boy in his thoughts. He never wanted to discuss the issue alone and wanted intervention or advice from an elderly person.

He decided to talk to his friend Shahid's mother. He would meet her and seek help in finding a suitable boy.

Abdullah went to Shahid's house. Zaineb was in the kitchen when Abdullah knocked the door.

-   Good Morning, Abdullah said,
-   Same to you, Zaineb replied.

She was surprised to see him and worried if he has come to ask for the financial help again.

-   Shahid is not in the house, she said.
-   No, I have come to meet you and talk.—can I come?
-   Yes, indeed come in—I will get tea for you.
-   No, not required—I need your help and guidance.

Zaineb thought it must be money, and he is taking advantage of Shahid's absence.

-   It is Shabana. She is now of marriageable age, and need help to find a suitable boy.

Zaineb was bit relieved of immediate danger—but marriage—it will certainly need more funds.

-   You know, how is Shabana?
-   What do you mean? Worried Abdullah asked.
-   Shabana is outspoken, has many friends and looks at life from different points of view. She is indeed beautiful but has different ideas on life. She wants richness of life.—We have to find a suitable rich boy for her—have you spoken to her? Has Sharifa spoken to her?"

This shocked Abdullah. She knows Shabana well and Sharifa never told him this. He cursed Sharifa

No, we have not spoken, and that is the reason I came to seek help.

-   You speak to Shabana first, and get her ideas.
-   Will you call Shabana and have a conversation. This will help me?
-   Yes, I can, if she is willing to talk.

- Do you know Sajjad? Son of Inayat?—They are not rich people and a large family. Sajjad is a talented boy—I can talk to his mother and find out what she has to say.
- No, I don't know them may be Sharifa knows. I will find out.
- But you first speak to Shabana and then I will talk to Sajjad's mother—oh! I forgot you wanted me to speak to her first. OK ask her to see me if you can or else I will get time to come there and meet her. I think this will be better as Sharifa will be there, and it will help me too.
- Thank you and I will leave now. Give my salaams to Shahid.

He left, but the visit made him more worried.

Shabana, Shabana what he has to do?

CHAPTER 23

It was evening time and Iqbal was sitting in his room thinking of his meeting with Hamid.

He was clear in his mind that if the topic of the book is raised he will take the blame.

The story was—"that he had come to the house to meet Tabassum in the morning, but she was not in the house. Zaheda asked him to wait and he saw the book in the room while aunty was in the kitchen making the tea. He was sorry and asked for pardon and will convince that he has not even discussed this book with anyone."

He memorised the whole idea and wanted to be sure that it was an excellent idea and had no loop holes. After many revisions, he realised there was a loop hole.

The weakness was that he had no rational reason to be at the house at that time. He had to find a strong compelling argument for it.

After few thinking shots—he thought of aunt Shabana. He wanted to tell that Shabana sent him as she wanted to meet Tabassum. But why? He could not find the compelling reason.

"What if Hamid uncle asks Shabana?" Oh that could be a big problem. His mother will come to know and never wanted mother to get involved.

He dropped the idea. He remembered his mother had told him to pray a D'oa in difficulty, and seek guidance from Allah. He was not willing to pray that D'oa as convinced that he was at fault and Allah had to punish him for what he had done.

But his faith took over, and he prayed. He closed his eyes and was waiting for guidance from heaven.

The answer came. His faith became stronger. His belief in mother became even stronger. The reason was simple

He had come to collect the book of Q'uran translation from him as he wanted to read it. Tabassum had told him that a translation was available with him.

This will involve me and him. Tabassum not involved, and there was no question of him suspecting now.

He dressed up and told Sharifa that he was going to meet Hamid uncle as he had called. Sharifa asked to convey greetings to the family.

He had arranged with Tabassum to be away and not available in the house when he comes.

He walked with fear, anxiety and knocked the door. Zaheda opened and welcomed him.

After the greetings, she asked him to be seated and informed Hamid.

Hamid came to the room, holding the postcard in hand. He had decided to use the same as trump card and see the reaction of Iqbal on seeing the postcard, which could give him the idea of him seeing the book.

Iqbal saw the postcard and remembered it that it was the same which was in that book. There was a striking red colour spot in the corner which he had seen while glancing the book. He was convinced that it was the same, and he was being tested.

Zaheda walked in with tea and saved him from his nervousness. He determined to be brave and avoid any indication of seeing the book unless asked.

Zaheda's involvement relieved him.

Zaheda started praising him for his love and being so obedient to Sharifa and taking care of her. She praised for his study skills which Tabassum narrated and told why Hamid had called. Hamid wanted to help to get a decent job.

Was this the reason? Why then the postcard? He mumbled.

Though he was confused, but bit relieved now. He thought Zaheda's involvement was Allah's grace and forgiveness. He got his courage back.

Hamid was irritated with Zaheda's involvement.

She was taking the game away from him.

He wanted to be alone with Iqbal and was now not even able to ask her to go out. There was no reason for it. She had even brought her cup of tea and wanted to be a part of the conversation.

Zaheda had a specific reason for it, she was afraid that Hamid may not treat Iqbal well and may create unwanted situation and wanted to be sure that Hamid intends to help him. She had asked Tabassum to stay away from the house. This was a blessing for Tabassum as she had to be away anyhow as per the plan of Iqbal.

Zaheda asked Iqbal final exam's result and what the plans were for the future.

This relieved Iqbal. He said that he was looking for a respectable job, was ready for hard work required for it, be honest and dedicated to work and wanted to help and relieve Sharifa from any hardship in her life. He wanted to send Sharifa for Haj pilgrimage.

Hamid's frustration and anger melted away.

He went inside and came back with a notebook and pen. The postcard was missing. Iqbal noted it and was extremely relieved. Hamid asked Iqbal to write his name, address, qualifications in the notebook. He told Iqbal that he could get a decent job for him if he wanted it.

He then talked Iqbal's reading habit. Which book he read? what his knowledge on Islamic subjects was?

Iqbal replied Hamid queries with clarity and dignity and the meeting ended well. The fear of dirty book did not appear anywhere. Still he had no idea, why the postcard was in the hands of Hamid.

Iqbal's fear continued, but took permission to leave.

On the way back, he thought of teasing Tabassum. He had now got hold over her. He now wanted to meet, tease, question and embrace her. His dreams came gushing like rain of flood water. His body was tense, and spirits high.

CHAPTER 24

Shabana and Hasmukh were sitting on a beach.

- It is no point getting upset, Hasmukh was saying.
- I have to; my brother is now looking for a boy.
- The same is true at my house. In fact, they arranged a meeting on next Sunday, and I meet the girl.
- Will you go then?
- I have to, else it will be difficult. But I can always refuse.
- That is fine, but it does not solve our problem. My brother will kill me if he finds our relationship
- I don't see any other reason but to run away.
- Where can we run away? Where shall we go? Who will support us? From where we will get money to live?
- You don't worry. My father has plenty of black money lying in the house. I will steal something from there.
- Are you sure you can do that? There is no money in our house. You know how we are managing. My brother is always struggling. My sister-in-law works to support him. I hate poverty. They had no money for my higher study. He wants me to get a job and help him. I honestly hate this status of my life. I want to live happily, enjoy the luxury of life. Will you give me this my dear? I love you.
- Yes, indeed, I love you too.

He pulled Shabana near and kissed her. She was always willing to submit and give him the full advantage of her body. It was getting dark, and they hide themselves behind the rock. With a long kiss and intense grip, he held her in his complete control. She ran out of breadth and released herself from the grip.

- So now let us decide on the plan how to go ahead.
- Yes, I agree. Will you run away with me?
- I have no other choice. I know it will be an enormous blow to my brother, but I cannot help it.
- Ok then let me think. But now I want to enjoy you. Give me a passionate kiss.
- Now that is enough for today. Let us go. If I reach home late I have to give explanations, and I don't like it.
- One more time, I am still hungry.
- You can after marriage. I will show you then what I am.

She wanted to get up, but Hasmukh pulled her back and now the embrace was with the strength.

She finally released herself from his grip, got up, and arranged her dress properly.

Hasmukh got up, and they walked to the bus stop. Shabana's bus arrived, she waved and went away.

CHAPTER 25

Sunday Hasmukh's parents have had arranged a visit to the girl's house for a preliminary meeting. Hasmukh had no choice but to go with them.

On reaching there, they had a traditional welcome and exchange of thoughts. The girl was not present, and Hasmukh had anxious time.

Finally, the waiting period was over. The parents asked Rashmi to join. She came and sat quietly.

Father wanted them to discuss and question each other and they were left alone in the room.

- What is your name? Hasmukh had to break the silence. He knew her name still the question came out of its own.
- Rashmi, she said quietly.
- My name is Hasmukh
- Yes, I know.
- What are you doing, now?
- Nothing much.
- What! I was told that you are working in a bank.
- Yes, I do but that is not worth mentioning it.
- Oh! So you don't enjoy your work.
- No, I do appreciate it, but it depends what you call happiness.
- I don't understand what you are saying.
- Not my fault.

Hasmukh was now feeling uncomfortable and wanted to close the meeting.

- It seems you are not ready for this meeting, he said.
- Yes, I don't want to get married now, but the parents don't listen.

- You just tell them and settle the matter.
- It is not that simple. Can we meet somewhere else and I will tell you more.
- Where?
- Say to-morrow near our railway station at 6 PM.

Please don't talk to anyone. I treat you as a friend and will be honest with you. Will you come and meet me?

- I will be a trustworthy friend so let us meet to-morrow.

She went away from the room and Hasmukh wondering what had happened.

The parents walked in and looked at Hasmukh. They were not sure what happened between them.

- She is extremely friendly and charming, the father said
- Yes, I like her and want her to be my daughter-in-law, the mother said.
- Did you like her?
- This is the first meeting, and I cannot answer so early. She needs time to think., Hasmukh replied.
- Yes, let the children take their time. It is a matter of their life. Our times were different-the parents were deciding everything, the father laughed and said.

It was time to say good bye, and they left happily.

Hasmukh was looking eagerly for tomorrow's meeting.

He was not sure whether he should discuss this with Shabana, who was keen to know the outcome of the meeting. He cannot avoid her and had to meet and explain.

They met at their usual place. Shabana was in best dress. She was looking sexy and Hasmukh had difficulty in controlling the emotions. Shabana knew it well and wanted to exploit his desires.

- She is extremely sweet looking and I like her! Hasmukh teased her.
- Oh so now I am no one for you.
- What can I do, the parents are forcing me? They are rich, and I am getting a respectable dowry.

Shabana was now anxious. Is she going to lose him? Is he telling the truth or teasing? She went near holding his hand. Hasmukh knew now she was his and grabbed her. The crowded place; and the sun were still in the last phase of journey. In this light, Shabana was more desirable, and he could not control himself. He dragged her behind a parked lorry and kissed. It was intense, and she submitted to him.

On releasing her, he found tears in her eyes.

- Why tears in your eyes?
- They are of happiness that you still love me.
- I always loved you and will always love you.
- But now you have found a rich girl, your parents are forcing, so what can you do.
- No, don't worry, I am yours.

Hasmukh then told her what had happened and Rashmi wanted to meet to-morrow evening. He is meeting her and planning to take Shabana and introduce her. Shabana was bit satisfied and looked forward to meeting. She wanted to go, but Hasmukh wanted her to stay. It was still not dark enough to go and sit behind the rock and enjoy her. Shabana knew his intentions but wanted to keep him waiting and waiting. She wanted to evaluate her position in life and look forward to to-morrow's meeting. She insisted to go and went away, leaving Hasmukh with his unfulfilled desire.

They both had a sleepless night.

Finally the day came, and Hasmukh went to the railway Station at the appointed time. Shabana was with him, but he asked her to stay away.

He saw Rashmi from a distance, and had a young man with her. Rashmi waived, and he responded.

- He is my Parsi friend Jahangir. He works with me at the Bank.
- Nice to meet you. I am Hasmukh. What a coincidence I have a friend with me.

He waived at Shabana and called her.

- She is Shabana, my childhood friend.
- Nice to meet you too.

Rashmi was bit upset with the presence of Shabana. She took Hasmukh aside.

- Why she is here.
- I was not expecting Jahangir
- I have a reason to bring him. He is my boy friend and plan to marry.

This was a surprise but a pleasant one and relieved him of the worries.

- She is my childhood friend and wanted to see you. He just lied.
- Is she your childhood friend? only friend?, she said sarcastically.

She said let us go to cafe and discuss what I have to say.

On reaching the Cafe, they sat in one corner table.

- Hasmukh, now you know what I want in life.
- Yes, but how can I help you, I will tell my parents that I did not like you.
- No, that is not going to solve problem.
- I want my parents to be happy that I have selected the boy of their choice. They will not then bother me with other boys.
- What have I to do then?
- We will be friends—get engaged and pretend to stay engaged.
- How is that possible?
- Why not—you flirt with Shabana and I with Jahangir. Life will be steady for both of us.
- Yes, an excellent idea, and it will allow us the time to find the right solution, Jahangir intervened.
- We are planning to run away, but Jahangir needs time, and I need your help, Rashmi said
- How much time you need, Hasmukh asked.
- About six months, Jahangir said.
- Ok then done. I will help you, Hasmukh said.

Hasmukh thought this to be a God sent help in arranging his eloping with Shabana.

- But if your parents ask for engagement ceremony? Then will you do that? Shabana asked.
- Yes, if we have to do that drama, we do it, Rashmi replied.
- Please return my engagement ring, she said to Hasmukh laughingly.
- You return my ring too, and they laughed.

They had a fantastic time.

They thought that they had a master plan to fool parents.

They thought that they could do whatever they want in life.

Only Shabana was silent and tense.

CHAPTER 26

Tabassum returned home with lots of fear and excitement. Iqbal had gone, and the parents were chitchatting and laughing.

- What is it Mom, why so happy?
- Indeed, Hamid is going to help Iqbal in finding a decent job.
- Oh I am so happy. Will it make him rich?
- No job can make you rich, Hamid intervened. But will give respect in life and society, and then one has to find the way to progress and become rich.
- Iqbal is smart and hardworking, I am sure he will become rich, Tabassum said.
- Why are you worried? Zaheda intervened?
- Iqbal is my childhood friend, I know how Sharifa aunt struggled for his education. I want Iqbal to be rich and get everything missed so far. I like him, Mom.

The words were a bombshell for both. Tabassum did not realise what she blurted out and ran away.

Hamid was angry.

- Did you hear what she said?
- Yes,—I heard, but don't be serious. She has a soft corner. Iqbal is childhood friend, and wants him to be happy.
- Don't fool yourself. If you are not going to handle Tabassum, then I will have to do something.
- Don't get upset, I will find out more.
- Yes, do it fast and I don't want Iqbal now to be near her. I will talk to Abdullah and warn him.

- Please be patient and be careful.
- Yes, I have to find out Ashraf's intentions. They are waiting for answer. You have to tell Tabassum, I am serious, and will not accept any non-sense.

The situation was tense in the room. Tabassum realised this when came back after changing the dress and hugged Zaheda. Hamid did not look and ignored her.

- Can you come in the kitchen? I need help. Zaheda wanted to tell the seriousness of the situation and wanted her to stay away from Iqbal

When in kitchen, Zaheda wanted to know more of their relationship.

- Hamid is arranging a meeting with Ashraf so that you two can meet and understand each other better.
- I told you mom, I am not interested, and don't want to get married now. I need to finish education. Why so much hurry for the marriage?
- You don't get decent boys. They are rich and well settled family, and we don't want to miss this opportunity. We have a daughter, and have to fulfil the responsibility. It is our duty to get you happily married.
- Allah says not to force marriage on a woman and has given a full right to her. No one can marry her till she says on her own free will and agrees for marriage. This is written in Q'uran. Why are you forcing it on me?

Zaheda regretted having involved Allah. Tabassum was right. Zaheda never knew that her naughty daughter was so knowledgeable.

- You are right. She conceded. But you have responsibility to obey your parents and obey their instructions and follow their decisions. You are still a child. You don't know what Life is? In our times, we just obeyed our parents.
- I obey you, but times have changed you have to respect children's views. I want to study and don't want to get married now.
- Are you in love with someone? Zaheda could not resist and had to ask her.

Tabassum was shocked by this direct question.

- What No Mom, What are you talking? Are you worried? Iqbal, yes, I like him but have not even thought marriage. He is my childhood friend and enjoy his company. I want to study and then decide. When I decide I will first tell you. You are my mother. I need your help. Please tell Dad to listen. I beg you.

- Zaheda was shocked by this open declaration of her daughter. A different character of her daughter was emerging. She had known her only as a playful and flamboyant daughter, but could sense the impact of Iqbal on her thoughts.

Zaheda was not sure how Hamid can be convinced of Tabassum's dreams. The milk in the kitchen boiled and overflowed. Tabassum ran and put off the stove.

Tabassum hugged Zaheda.

Zaheda was quiet and had tears in eyes. Tabassum as usual used the duppatta to wipe tears.

Mother and daughter held in an embrace.

There was a voice heard from the door.

- I am going to Amanullah's house and will be late.

Hamid left the house.

CHAPTER 27

Iqbal was loitering on the road and was expecting Tabassum to be there. Today she was not there at usual time and this worried him.

It was getting dark, and he thought something must be wrong and decided to go to her house.

On knocking the door, Zaheda opened the door and surprised to see Iqbal.

- What is it, why you are here at this time?
- Oh I need to give these papers to Hamid Uncle. Is he at home?

His eyes were looking for Tabassum. Zaheda sensed his searching eyes and wanted to take this opportunity.

Tabassum was crying in her room, knowing that her father has gone to Ashraf's house. She had heard Iqbal's voice but did not want to face him and decided not to go out at this time.

- Iqbal you are a remarkably close friend of Tabassum, and you both know each other since childhood. Is this not true?
- Yes, Aunty I am. Anything wrong? Is Tabassum not at home?
- Well you know how difficult it is for parents whose daughter is young and of marriageable age.
- I do but what that has to do with us. I don't understand it.
- I need your help. Will you help me?
- Yes, indeed I will always help you. You helped us so much. My mother has always told me your goodness.
- Do you know Ashraf?, the son of Subedar Family.
- No, I don't know him. I never met.
- They are rich people and approached us for Tabassum.

- What?

Iqbal felt as if the ground had slipped under his feet. His head was dizzy, and he felt as if the energy from body had vanished. His face was reflecting the state of his inner thoughts.

Zaheda realised the state of Iqbal's mind and wanted to take full advantage of it.

- Are you not happy?
- Yes, Indeed I am, Iqbal uttered shakily.
- Then you must help me. Tabassum is not agreeing and wants to continue her studies.
- In a way she is right, she is brilliant and must complete the studies.
- We are not asking her to stop the studies. We will have the engagement, and then she can continue the studies.
- I don't think after getting engaged, she will be able to pursue the studies. It is hard, I guess.
- Hamid wants her to meet Ashraf and then decide, but she is refusing to meet. What is wrong in meeting him? But she is refusing, and Hamid is upset and may do something wrong. Can you help me by talking to Tabassum? Can you convince her for a meeting with Ashraf?
- I can try but where is she? He fumbled while speaking.

There was a knock on the door and Hamid entered the house. On seeing Iqbal he lost his composure.

- What are you doing in my house at this time?
- Uncle I came to give you the papers you asked for and discuss future plans. I am grateful for your help.
- What plans?—I have nothing for you.
- Uncle you gave me so much hope. I depend on you to accomplish something in my life. I thought Allah sent me an Angel in you.

Zaheda intervened.

- No No, uncle will certainly help you. But he cannot make your future. It is you who have to work it out. Allah and your mother's prayers will be always with you. Uncle will help you.
- Can I leave the papers here for you to see.

Iqbal was now nervous.

- Are you serious? Are you willing to sacrifice something to get something? Remember in life nothing is free and everything has a price. Are you willing to pay that price? I am serious, and I want to help you.

- Whatever you say Uncle, I am willing to do it.
- OK—then you come with your mother and meet me on Sunday after midday prayers. That is after five days.—Leave the papers here and go.

Iqbal left but determined to meet Tabassum to resolve and get her views.

- I met Amanullah, and they are eager to do the engagement ceremony next month. They intend to visit us with the proposal. Hamid said to Zaheda.
- But why so much hurry, I discussed with her. She wants to study and does not want to get married.
- I am not talking of marriage. This is final, and nothing can stop it. Tell your daughter to behave and obey.
- We are doing wrong things. We are pushing our daughter to revolt— to do something which we only will repent.
- If you can't tell her and control her, then I need to take action. From today, she is not going to go out of the house without my permission. Where is she? I will tell her.
- She is in her room. I talked to her. There is nothing between her and Iqbal. They are just childhood friends and respect each other.
- Childhood friendship ends with the childhood. They are now not children. I don't believe that non-sense.
- On Friday, I will meet Sharifa so that she does not carry false dreams and notions.

Tabassum came from the room dressed up and told Zaheda

- Mom I am going to Sharifa aunt's house as she is going to teach me how to stitch formal dresses.

No, you are not going anywhere. Hamid got up, held her hand, dragged her and locked her in the room.

It happened in a flick of a second.

Zaheda dumfounded.—Hamid furious.

Tabassum was crying and thought she has lost the loving father.

95

Chapter 28

Shabana and Hasmukh met at their usual place. They had decided to run away and wanted to finalise their plan and strategy.

- Are you sure we can handle it?, Shabana asked.
- I have not done it before, so I don't know, Hasmukh said laughingly.
- You are always joking and not taking the matter seriously. Legally we both are adults so nobody can stop us. But how and where go and live then?
- My father has cash in the house, even if I take some of it he will not notice. The key of the cupboard is always with my mother, and I can manage.
- I am sorry I cannot do that. There is no cash in the house. My bhabhi has some jewellery, which I can steal if you want.
- Yes, we need that, and you have to take it.
- Let me see what I can get.

The matter is too serious, and I have to relieve my tension, Hasmukh pulled her and kissed. Shabana was tensed and not in the mood but could not resist. After a few minutes of lip locks, they separated.

- I am impatient; we go out to-night and enjoy ourselves.

Shabana was silent which was taken by him as her consent.

- I have planned and booked a room in the hotel and paid for it. You must come and let us celebrate our wedding night.
- We are not married yet
- So what!, that is some protocol to be performed by a priest, this is between you and me.

- But it is a sacred thing, and without performing it, we will be doing an immoral act. I will not do it till I am your wedded wife.
- We are running away, we won't have the wedding ceremony, we won't receive blessings of any one
- You want to have your rituals performed. It is between you and me only, and we have to satisfy our dream when we like.
- Still I want to come to you as your wedded wife.
- So you won't come. Ok then I will not satisfy your wish and will not run away with you.
- I knew, you will say that. You don't need love of a woman. What you are after is sex only.
- For men, pleasurable sex is true love only.
- We are drifting away from our primary objective. We came here to plan our running away and when to do it.
- For your information today I cannot marry you. It is not possible, it is my monthly period.
- Good Excuse you women have!!!

They finally decided that it will be on Saturday. Shabana will take whatever she can from the house and go to Rashmi's house. Hasmukh will come and meet there.

They will then take a bus to Pune. Rashmi's friend arranged a priest and a hotel. The marriage ceremony will be according to the Hindu rites, and they will become husband and wife.

Shabana had no choice but to accept this arrangement. Her dream of having a Nikah Ceremony performed was not practical and possible. She accepted it as her fate.

Finally, the dreadful day arrived. Shabana gathered the courage and took the jewelleries of Sharifa quietly and walked away when Sharifa had gone for work. Hasmukh came with a pile of suitcase. They bid farewell to Rashmi, who had cooperated whole heartedly in the plan and provided the moral support.

On the way to Pune, Shabana was nervous, shivering and sometimes wondering why she was giving such punishment to the family—to the brother—to the sister-in-law who have been so kind to her and what will happen to them. Will Allah forgive her—the thoughts came and disappeared.

Hasmukh was wondering what will happen to his mother. Will she be able to bear this pain? He was not sure, why he had to do this? Why parents don't listen to their children and fulfil their desire? Why society is so cruel and unfair to them? The thoughts came and disappeared.

The trip to Pune was silent for both of them. The thrill and excitement of running away was fading away.

On reaching Pune, Hasmukh's friends organised the things in a proper manner. The priest a young man performed the marriage, Hashmukh and Shabana took the required oath. Few invited friends shared the fun and excitement of the runaway marriage.

Finally, the long awaited wedding night came.

Shabana renamed as Shuhana.

CHAPTER 29

Sharifa was worried.

Iqbal went to look for Shabana as it was approaching midnight and had not returned.

Abdullah was away from home on outdoor duty.

Iqbal came back searching for every possible place known where Shabana should be, but there was no evidence.

- Mom tried everywhere. Should inform the Police?
- No, wait for Abdullah to be here. Shabana might have informed, and he has not informed me. Now everyone whom you visited knows and will become an unnecessary gossip issue.
- Mom you are right. I had one place in mind, but did not go there.
- Where?
- Hasmukh's house with whom she was so close.

This was a bombshell for Sharifa.

Hasmukh!!—Hasmukh!—Hasmukh!

Sharifa trembled, the confused mind got flooded with so many issues, and she could not take it. The pressure started taking its toll. She sat in a chair.

- Get a glass of water.

Iqbal ran and brought a glass of water. While handing over the glass, felt the shakiness of mother's hand. The whole body was shivering.

- Are you ok? Don't worry too much; wait for Dad to come and everything will be right. Should I make a call to Hasmukh's house, just to find it?

- No, it is too late to call, wait till Abdullah comes and takes care of it. Go to sleep. It is midnight and time for prayer so let me pray.
- No, I will be here—you finish prayers.

Sharifa went for prayer abulation.

Iqbal went to room to bring the book which he was reading—"How to Test your Love". Tabassum was in mind, after the talk with Zaheda. Iqbal wanted to meet Tabassum and find out more.

After the prayers, Sharifa went to check Shabana's room and noticed that the cupboard was empty. Her heart tumbled with fear.

- Iqbal, she shouted.

Iqbal came running. What is it?

- Look, Shabana has run away from the house, and took all her belongings. What answer I will give to Allah. I did not care, and Allah punished for carelessness
- She crumbled and started crying. Iqbal was stunned.

Terrified Iqbal did not know how to help the crying mother at this time.

- Holding mother in arms, made her sleep on bed and sat next to her.

Iqbal knew nothing how to handle the situation at this hour of the night.

There was a knock at the door.

Thinking it is Shabana, Iqbal ran to open the door.

Sharifa got the sense and hoping it is Shabana, she became alert.

Where is my son? Is the idiot hiding here?

Himmatbhai, Hasmukh's father entered the house with a thunder. The loud voice terrified Sharifa and Iqbal.

- He is not here, and we have no idea.
- Where is that rascal sister of yours? She has spoiled my son and I will see that she pays for what she has done. Where is she? He shouted.
- She has gone to friend's house; Iqbal could not find any other excuse.
- Friend's house? Do you think I am an idiot? Tell the truth or else I go to Police and file a complaint. She has stolen five lakhs of Rs from my house and run away.

Sharifa gathered the courage,

- We have no idea—where she has gone. We are worried and waiting for her. Abdullah is out on a business trip and expected tomorrow. I think we both are victim of children's foolishness.

Himmat became silent He could see the worry and pain on the face of Sharifa. He could see the innocence on the face of Iqbal.

- I am afraid they have run away from the city. They have taken 5 lakhs of Rs from the cupboard. Before they behave stupid and nonsense, I have to catch them. Did you check your house?
- Uncle, we don't have money in house. Iqbal intervened. Yes, the cupboard is empty, the dresses are gone.
- Are you sure? No jewelleries.

This thought shocked Sharifa.

- She went to her room. The moment she opened cupboard, she knew what had happened.

The jewellery box was not there.

- No everything is ok; she has not taken any jewellery.
- She kept control on speech. She was lying, and it was against her morals.
- Well than I have to go to Police and report.

If they do wrong, I am going to kill them. I cannot tolerate any nonsense. I am warning you, take care of her. I know how to manage my son and bring him back. I will see you tomorrow when your husband is back, and I am again warning you.

Himmat went away leaving the annoyance and anger in the atmosphere of the room.

- Shabana has taken away the jewelleries, Sharifa said to Iqbal.
- What!—Mom, you said she has not.
- I had to lie. I had to protect her. I know my Allah will not forgive.
- HE Will—HE knows your situation—HE gave you the courage to speak lie. HE will forgive. HE has forgiven

Iqbal got hold of Sharifa and led her to the room, sat next to her and was thinking

How to face Himmatbhai and his anger?

How to face Abdullah when he arrives?

How to save Sharifa from the embarrassment and suffering?

The night took over and both mother and son were silent and watching each other.

Sharifa was thinking of jewelleries and thanked Allah that she did not bring the diamond necklace, which Maimuna left for Iqbal's wife.

- Mom shall I inform Nana, he will come and help.
- No, wait till Abdullah returns and resolves the issue. He did not listen to me. You go to sleep, it is late and we have to face tomorrow.
- You take the rest; I will be sleeping here . . .
- No, go to sleep, I want to read Q'uran.
- Read Q'uran, I will stay here only.

The exhaustion took over Iqbal, and he could not keep awake.

Sharifa was reading Q'uran and wanted peace in mind which was full of turmoil and torment.

The morning Azan Prayer was heard. Sharifa went for prayer abulation and woke up Iqbal to perform the prayer. After prayer, she prepared tea for both.

Iqbal could not control his disturbed sleep and went to room to sleep again.

The Knock at the door shook him.

Himmat was at the door with Police.

- It is her daughter who has stolen money from the house and made my son run away. She knows where they are? Arrest her and she will speak out.
- Calm down and let me do the job, the officer said.
- I am the sub-inspector Arvind from the Police Station. I have come to investigate the complaint of Himmat, and you have to tell the truth. If you lie and try to evade police, you will have to pay a terrible price of it. It could be jail for both. So please tell the truth.
- The truth is we don't know. My aunty has not come home since yesterday night; Iqbal spoke with firm and powerful voice. That is the truth nothing but the truth. We are suffering, and have sympathy with Himmat Uncle. My father is out of Mumbai on office work and is expected today or tomorrow. We don't know what Himmat uncle is referring to. We only know that aunt Shabana and Hasmukhbhai were friends and have nothing more to say.

Iqbal's composure and control impressed Arvind.

- The boy is telling the truth, and I can only write the statement. We will examine the same and then only can take further action, Arvind said to Himmat.

- What are you saying now? Himmat shouted. You told at the Police station that you would arrest and put them behind jail to find out the truth.

- Yes, true but only after I find out the truth. Let me finish my job.

Arvind recorded the statement of Iqbal, and took signature.

- I understand what you have told me in the statement is true. You have my sympathies too. Now, if you get any information about Shabana or Hasmukh you have to inform me. If you hide, you will be involving yourself in the crime. Please consider my words and obey the instructions. I expect you to abide by the law and help police.

Himmat was angry.

- I am not finished with you people yet, he looked at Iqbal.

Arvind warned Himmat and asked him to behave.

- You are threatening them in front of a police officer. I can understand your frustration as father. But you are the father of a son. Their suffering is more. It is their daughter if she is involved.

- She is involved, shouted Himmat and went away.

Sharifa was crying and hiding the face.

CHAPTER 30

The arrival of Police created news in the building. The inquisitiveness spread and everyone wanted to find out what happened.

The gossip outside the door continued.

- That girl was like that only!
- What will happen now to Abdullah?
- A blot on the family!
- Sharifa's fault, she did not take care.
- Why did they not marry her?
- The fault of education.
- If my daughter had done it, I kill her.

The comments were endless.

Zaheda heard the news and wanted to meet Sharifa, but Hamid was dead against it.

- Don't want to meet, Hamid said.
- Sharifa is in trouble, her husband is not there, and it is our duty to help in this difficult time.
- Now, I am more worried for Tabassum.
- Trust Tabassum, she is not like that
- Don't need to trust anyone. I like her to get married. I don't like Iqbal to meet her now, and you take care of that. This is a stern warning to both of you.

Hamid left for the office.

Tabassum was listening, came to Zaheda and hugged.

- Mom, go and meet Sharifa aunty, she needs the help.
- Did you hear what your father said?

- He is angry and worried. I told you mom, Iqbal is a friend, and I like him. There is nothing more than that. Don't you trust your daughter?
- I do, but if you want to help them, you will not come with me.
- I will go alone and meet. Hamid will become angry, but will manage that.
- Yes, Mom, I promise, please go and meet Sharifa aunty.

Zaheda was not sure of her daughter's promise, but wanted to go and meet Sharifa.

Zaheda came to Sharifa's house, knocked, and Iqbal opened the door.

- Please come in and sit, I will go and inform her. How is Hamid Uncle.? I wanted to meet him for the job, and this happened. Mother is worried, confused and crying. Please help her. How is Tabassum? Really she is so upset; I have not seen her since last so many days.

Sharifa came from the room, had tears in eyes and hugged Zaheda.

- Allah is not pleased and is punishing me. I honestly don't know what to do.
- Be patient. HE is testing the courage. This HE always does with whom HE loves more.
- Where is Abdullah? Any news of Shabana?
- I don't know. Abdullah is supposed to come today. Shabana we can't tell. Hasmukh, her friend has also run away from the house. Hasmukh's father was here and blamed for what has happened, he even came with a Police Officer. Can Hamidbhai help?

This was a shock for Zaheda. Sharifa was expecting Hamid to help and Hamid?. She was stunned and speechless.

- Yes, we are with you and do what is required, but cannot fight against the law. I hope and pray that Shabana is safe and has not done wrong against the law.
- The conscious tells that she has married him, Sharifa said.
- What?—Zaheda could not control the intensity of her voice. Did you know it then?
- I suspected it and told Abdullah, he was looking for a good boy, but now this happened.

Iqbal came with the tea and biscuits.

- Aunty, please take it, and my mom will have it with you, she has not eaten since yesterday night.
- Thanks Iqbal, but this was not required. I had the breakfast but will give company to Sharifa.

Sharifa could not refuse Zaheda and had tea with her.

- Did you inform Masoodbhai? He can help you in this difficult time. Inquired Zaheda.

- No, waiting for Abdullah to come and then decide what to do. The concern is now Shabana and Hasmukh.

- Then let us wait till he comes. Hamid has left for office, and is not aware of this situation in detail. I will talk and see how he can help. I will leave now, but take care, and if needed please do call.

- Aunty, thanks for your kind thoughts, Iqbal said. When do I come to meet Hamid uncle for the job? I need the help and advice. Can you ask Tabassum to meet me? I need to share few things with her.

- I will tell Hamid, and he will see how to help you. Tabassum will not be able to see you now. There is proposal of marriage for Tabassum. The family is good and rich people. It is not proper that now she gets involved in any social rumours. I hope you understand and will help her by not meeting. You are her childhood friend and must not do any harm. I hope you understand what I am saying.

- No, I don't. Tabassum is indeed my dear friend and I will not hurt her.

- Sharifa can explain better, though may be difficult to understand. The issues faced by parents of a girl are many. I thank you for your understanding. I will now go and will remind Hamid to help you. Hamid will certainly help you out. My prayers are with you.

Zaheda left—shattering the world of Iqbal.

Sharifa was trying to understand the meaning of Iqbal and Tabassum's relationship.

CHAPTER 31

Arrival of Abdullah did not bring any peace in the life of Sharifa. As usual had nothing to do except blame Sharifa for the miseries of life. He refused to go anywhere and help in search of Shabana.

On the news of Abdullah's arrival, a police man came and asked him to come to the police station. He had no choice and had to go.

He pleaded complete ignorance in the whole affair. He was equally ashamed of the whole episode, and if the sister faces him, he will shoot her. She was a disgrace to the family, and will not allow her to live peacefully.

Officer Arvind advised to calm down and told not to do any wrong thing. If any contact with the sister, he should inform the Police.

Abdullah, shattered and frustrated in life, wanted to run away from this situation. He went to mosque and sat alone in a corner. His eyes were wet. His heart was pulsating at a much higher pace. He was shattering and could not control frustration. He was seriously thinking of running away from here.

Sharifa and Iqbal were waiting for the return and then decide what to do next.

There was no sign of Abdullah and they started worrying.

- Go to police station and find out, Sharifa told Iqbal.

Iqbal was worried too and had to go to the Police Station.

- He has gone from here. We have simply recorded the statement and did not detain him here, the sub-inspector told Iqbal.
- He has not come home, and we are worried. Can you please help?
- Don't worry, where will he go? Check with friends. In this situation people go and drink to forget the things. Was he drinking?? Was his

friend's circle drinking? Go and find out there. We are sure he will be there.

- My father was not drinking, Iqbal retorted.
- Ya Ya, we know and they laughed.

With worry and anxiety, Iqbal walked back.

He heard somebody calling his name. He looked around but could not find any familiar person or friend nearby.

Iqbal I am Tabassum, I want to talk.

He was shocked with these words. A woman in a burqa came coming near to him.

- I am Tabassum; I am trying to meet. I am in Burqa as I don't want anybody to see me.
- Why like this? You are aware what has happened to our family.
- Yes, I heard. It is extremely unfortunate. How can I help?
- Nobody can help. We have to face it, but why in this dress?
- It is a long story. My father is arranging my marriage with Ashraf, that idiot. I want to study, but is not willing to listen.
- Yes, your mother told me and needs my help to convince you to accept the proposal.
- What! What!, my mother told you. How can she do this?
- What is wrong? They are parents and well wisher and want you to be happy.
- Yes, but I am their child, they have to listen and care for my happiness too. Now I don't have much time. My father has warned not to meet you. I cannot tell what the next step is. I want to meet peacefully and take your help.
- I am myself in real trouble, mother is shaken up, and I certainly don't know how I can help. But I am your friend, and will certainly do whatever I can. You please now go before somebody sees us.
- I am in Burqa; nobody will realise I am Tabassum. So when and where we can meet.
- I honestly cannot tell now but say day after tomorrow in the college library.
- No, I am not allowed to go anywhere. You please contact Sakina, and she will inform.
- OK, will do that.

Tabassum lifted the burqa and wanted to see Iqbal's face. It was not the Iqbal, she knew. She closed the burqa and had tears in the eyes.

The life was gone out of Iqbal—his strength was shattered, and he was not sure how to face mother without any news of Abdullah.

Iqbal reached home, Sharifa was waiting, and hugged Iqbal.

- He is not there mom; nobody knows where he has gone. Police are saying, look with friends.
- You dad has no fiends, he is alone in life. He is broken and cannot bear this. I cannot guess what he is going to do.

It was impossible to control and she cried.

Mom wait, he will come home. I have no idea where to search. Have you any idea?

- Go to shop, it will be still open. Maybe he is there.
- No mom, not there, I did pass by the shop, but it was closed. What shall we do? Can I ask Hamid uncle and seek the help.
- Yes, we can ask him. Let us wait. It is too late, and will not be nice to disturb them now.
- Should I then inform Nanaji?
- Yes, but wait for tonight. Go and take rest, I wish to pray.
- No, I will be here and you pray.

Abdullah was walking on the road, hiding the face in the darkness of night. He came to the railway station.

Before boarding the train, he bought an inland letter from the stall and started writing.

He wrote

"My beloved Sharifa."

His hands trembled, tears in eyes, he could not even recollect when he had last addressed Sharifa with these beautiful words. He just could not remember it. It was always cursing, abusing and fighting.

"I am fed up of life. I don't know what I am going to do. I cannot pardon Shabana—if I meet her I will kill her. Iqbal is a talented boy he will look after you well. I cannot tell you where I am going. Don't try to search me. Allah will protect you."

He closed the letter dropped it in the letter box.

He just jumped in the train, not knowing where the train was going. He decided to run away from the worries, to run away from the responsibilities.

He was a defeated person.

He had lost faith in himself.

He had lost faith in Allah.

CHAPTER 32

The night passed

Sharifa and Iqbal had hardly any sleep. They both knew that he has gone away and had no courage to face the truth.

In the night, thought of Tabassum disturbed Iqbal. He had to meet her.

Tabassum was not aware of what had happened to Iqbal.

Iqbal was keen on meeting Tabassum to find out more details. The events were multiplying. Shabana, Abdullah, Tabassum all were on his mind, and was equally concerned of Sharifa.

-   Please go and inform Nana, Sharifa asked Iqbal.
-   Yes, I do that and then go to Hamid uncle for immediate guidance.
-   Yes, do that but don't talk of Abdullah.
-   Yes, I understand.

Iqbal phoned and talked to Masood.

Masood listened carefully and never wanted to create panic and fear in Iqbal. Masood comforted him and informed that he is leaving today and reach there by tomorrow. Be brave, don't get confused and panic, and don't listen or talk to many people.

-   Should I talk to Hamid uncle?
-   Who is he? I don't know. Will he help or will only take advantage of the situation?
-   Hamid uncle is a decent man and is going to help to get a job. I was to meet and discuss the same, and this happened. He is the father of Tabassum, whom you know.
-   Ok tell, if you are comfortable.

I am preparing to come and will be there by tomorrow, Inshallah

Iqbal then went to Hamid's house. On seeing Iqbal, Hamid was worried.

- Why have you come? I told, when I find a job, I will call. Go now I have nothing more to add to it.
- No Uncle I need help. It is about my father Abdullah.
- What happened? Need money? I have nothing to give. He borrows money from everybody and then runs away, and now has sent you.

Iqbal controlled his anger and frustration.

- No, it is not that. He has not come back to the house. He returned home yesterday morning and was called by the police station to give the statement, but never came back. Police recorded the statement and let him go. They know nothing. I informed Nana, and he is on the way and be here tomorrow. I thought I would take your advice and guidance on what to do.

Zaheda and Tabassum were in the room and listening to what Iqbal was saying.

- Go inside and don't come out. Hamid shouted at Tabassum.

Tabassum looked at Iqbal and quietly went away.

- I certainly don't know, why Allah is testing Sharifa so much, Zaheda intervened.
- Listen Iqbal, I have deep sympathy with your family, but cannot help in this matter. This is a Police Issue, and they have to do something. First, file an official complaint of missing father, and then any further action can be taken. Wait till your Nana arrives and decide what to do.
- Hamid is right. Wait for a day, Zaheda said. I will come and talk to Sharifa.
- Not required Hamid said. Keep quiet and don't interfere too much.
- We are neighbours and they need our help. It will please Allah if we can be of any help.
- Leave your religious sentiments with you. These are police issues, and don't get involved in the investigation. There would be questioning. We don't have the time to go to the court and police station. First the girl Shabana and now Abdullah. Things are complicated. Who knows they both might have jointly planned something. There is an issue of Rs. Five lakhs involved. Stay away. Hamid said, angrily.
- You go and wait for nana to arrive; he told Iqbal and dragged him to the door.
- You are right, and I wait. Will you still look for the job and help? Life has now become more difficult, and need the job urgently.

- Yes, he will certainly help you, Zaheda said.

Iqbal went confused as he had seen a different face of Hamid.

The thought of Tabassum was pressing on his mind. Why he sent her back in the room.

Does he hate me?

Will he help me?

What will he do to Tabassum?

Should he contact Sakina as asked and meet her?

He reached home. Sharifa was eagerly waiting. Himmat was there again with the Police Officer Arvind.

- He has come, ask him, he knows where his father is? They have cheated my son and run away with 5 lacs Rs. Himmat blurted out the anger to the police officer Arvind.
- Is this true what he says, Arvind asked Iqbal.
- I don't know what he is talking. I have no idea. My father came home yesterday; he was called to the police station. He went and has not returned back. We are concerned. We wanted to file a complaint. I went to police station, but they advised to wait. They said he would come back.
- The matter is now more serious, and your father is involved. If you are not telling truth, you will get involved and arrested.
- Arrest him now. You have a search warrant, shouted Himmat.
- I have to search your house. This is the warrant.
- I don't know warrant. You are Police officer, and if you want to do it, please do it. We are not stopping you.
- Arvind was sure of the innocence, but had to perform the duty. He instructed his sub-ordinates to do the needful.

Half hour passed, and police found nothing.

Arvind again advised Iqbal to be careful, and if any communication is established with his father or aunty, he should tell the police.

Himmat was grumbling but was helpless.

Sharifa had stopped crying, realised that now she has to take control of the situation and resolve the issues.

Sharifa suddenly got the strength which she received at the time of mother's death and how she had handled the situation and looked after the father.

She now has to take care of Iqbal.

She wanted to wait for Masood to arrive.

CHAPTER 33

Iqbal was eager to meet Tabassum. He wanted to meet Sakina and find out what to do.

After the people had gone, there was calm, and he thought of Tabassum. Abdullah—Shabana had vanished from mind

Iqbal's silence was worrying Sharifa.

- This is a difficult time, but face the situation with courage. I am with you. Nana will be here and be with us. Be brave and accept it. Allah is with us—we have not done wrong. HE will take care of us, Sharifa said to Iqbal.

- Yes, mom, I am sure nothing will happen. I will take care. Can I go out and meet a friend?

Sharifa was worried.

- No, you can't go out now anywhere. Be in front of my eyes.

- Mom, I won't run away, and understand you're suffering. You have the courage to fight it out and I am your son, I will not betray. But I must go now.

- How long? And tell me where you are going. I must know it.

- I can't tell you, Mom.

- What shouted Sharifa? From where you learnt to hide things from mother? I have not taught you this. Are you now stepping in the footsteps of your father?

Iqbal had no courage to tell the truth and could understand her fear and worries.

OK, If you feet it that way I am not going anywhere. Tomorrow after Nana comes, you will have peace. Now can I help you in the kitchen so that you can prepare the food for us?

- Yes, you come with me in the kitchen.

She was thinking—

Where does Iqbal want to go?

Whom does he want to meet?

Why is he not telling me?

A thought stuck to her mind.

Is it Tabassum?—She was not sure, but she wanted to confirm

What would you like to eat, she asked Iqbal.

- No, I don't want to eat. You make whatever you want. I will eat little with you.

Somebody knocked at the door.

- Who is it? Has he come back? Sharifa got excited and ran to open the door.

It was Sakina.

- I need help from Iqbal. My brother Abid has fractured his leg, and I need Iqbal's help to take him to the doctor.

Iqbal, see what Sakina is saying. Go and help her, Sharifa asked Iqbal

The moment Iqbal saw Sakina; he knew it was Tabassum who has done this. He got ready.

Iqbal went, and Sharifa was just wondering. It happened so fast and quick that she did not even realised that something had gone wrong.

At Sakina's house, Tabassum was there. But it was a different Tabassum, not smiling, not laughing and not teasing.

- Iqbal I am sorry, my father did not treat you well.
- He did not treat you well too. I can understand his anger. What has happened in our family is not acceptable. But why I am made responsible for it.? I just cannot understand it.

Sakina left the room to leave them alone.

- He is arranging my marriage against my will!
- Yes, your mother told me and wanted my help to make you understand.
- My mother told you!—Tabassum was surprised—when did she tell you? How are you going to help her? What are you thinking?
- She told me when she came to meet my mother. She had heard the news of Shabana's running away. She wanted to meet and comfort

my mother. It was so polite and nice. But your father, he is so angry and upset.

- He is not bothered, but worried that I am refusing to marry that boy—that idiot Ashraf. He thinks that I am in love with you, and you are not rich.
- In love with me!—So sweet of you, Iqbal laughed.
- Please don't laugh. I am serious. You have to help me.
- How can I help you?
- Go and tell Ashraf that we are in love, and he should not marry me. You can certainly do this for me.
- Will it help?—If you say so then I do it?

Sakina entered the room with tea and biscuits. Please hurry, Iqbal should leave before Abid arrives. He is a big talker and may tell everyone. I don't want any gossips.

- Yes, you are right; I will now meet Ashraf and tell, Iqbal told Tabassum.
- Yes, but do it quickly.

CHAPTER 34

Masood and Shirin arrived.

Sharifa had nothing to add but cried. Iqbal gave the details to Masood and ask advice how to handle the situation.

- Do you see any connection between the two events? Iqbal asked.

Sharifa and Shirin were surprised at this new Iqbal's thought.

- How can you believe this? He was not the person to use the sister to run away with cash of Rs. Five lacs as claimed by Himmatbhai.
- No, Masood said, I fear Abdullah got nervous and could not bear the pressure of Shabana's action. He lost courage and decided to run away.
- But police views are different. Himmat uncle's complaint is viewed seriously and actions are taken.
- Police evaluate from different viewpoints and take action.

The bell rang, and the postman dropped the letter of Abdullah.

Iqbal saw it was from Abdullah and got excited.

- He has written a letter to you, mom.
- Please give it to me, Sharifa ran for it.

Everyone was excited, Sharifa took the letter and on reading the first line she could not control and ran to her room. She had not heard these loving words from her husband since ages.

Everyone shocked and surprised. Shirin went after her. She expected distressing news and wanted to be with her. Sharifa was crying—on seeing Shirin, Sharifa handed over the letter to her. The contents of the letter were clear.

Shirin came out.

- He is alive but has gone somewhere and has asked not to look for him.
- From where he has written this letter, Masood asked.
- Cannot say but it is from Mumbai only. He has posted the letter and gone away.
- Shall we inform the police? Iqbal asked.
- Yes, go and report the same.

Iqbal took the letter and was about to go.

- I want his letter to be given back to me, It is mine, and I don't want to give to Police, Sharifa said
- Yes, I will not give it to them, but police must know about it. We cannot hide the receipt of this letter from them.
- I will go and come back soon; I will not give them this letter without your consent.

Masood was trying to console Sharifa and was thinking what wrong he has done in this life that his daughter was suffering.

- I like to take Sharifa and Iqbal with us and keep them away from this atmosphere, Shirin said
- No, I cannot come. If, Abdullah decides to come back the door should be open. We will stay here only, Sharifa replied
- You are right, but I fear he will not come so soon. You need the rest, Shirin said.
- No, it is not advisable. Sharifa is right. She should not leave this place. This is Mumbai, people will soon forget, and get busy in life. Ours is a small village, and may become a talk of the town. The pain then continues for a long time, Masood said.
- We will stay here for more days and decide what to do. Let Iqbal come back.

On the way to Police Station, Iqbal was dreaming.

The dream continued.

Does Tabassum truly love me? Should he consider it serious or she is just finding a way to get out from the situation? What is love? How to measure it? The thought rolled back to the evening of the day. The day, Tabassum had shown him the book. The feelings in the night he experienced. Was that the love or just sexual infatuation? Does she feel the same?—Does she dream the same way he was dreaming. They were intimate friends. They had shared enjoyable moments in life. They had happy memories of the same. As a friend, he always helped her. Now is the time to help her. She does not want to get married and needs the help to convince Ashraf that she does not want to marry.But how? Will the plan work? Will Ashraf get convinced of love affair? Will he go away?

She is beautiful indeed, and she was again in front of the eyes. He wanted to enjoy her and went to a restaurant and order a cup of tea. He closed eyes and Tabassum was there, he experienced divine moments with her and resolved to help her. The resolve became stronger and stronger.

He visualised her, not as a friend

But as a lover—

As a woman—

As a wife.

- The tea sir, the waiter shook him.

The dream got disturbed.

He finished the tea and reached the Police Station. Inspector Arvind was there. He showed the letter received from Abdullah and asked to locate him. Arvind looked at the letter and the postal envelope.

- I want this to be handed over to us for further investigation, he told Iqbal
- Sir, my mother is not willing to part with this letter. For her, it is a valuable remembrance.
- I can understand her feelings, but if you give me the same. We can get the testing done and find out from the postal stamp and may be able to locate him. I am not hundred percent sure, but it can be done. So talk to her.
- I have told her that I will not give the letter to police and bring it back. I must convince her and get her consent.
- I can certainly force you and keep this letter, but I respect her feelings—go and convince her. If needed, I will try to return it back after investigation.

Iqbal came home and explained everything to Sharifa and Masood. Finally, they convinced Sharifa to part with the letter. Iqbal took the photocopy, and went to Police Station to give the original. Arvind thanked him on good decision.

CHAPTER 35

Hameed was eager to complete the engagement ceremony and asked Zaheda to organise the same.

- I want to keep it simple and don't wish to make it very elaborate., He said to Zaheda
- She is the only daughter, and we must do it in the proper manner acceptable and respectable. Zaheda responded.
- Yes, but keep it simple.
- I asked her but is not ready for it and does not want to talk. She firmly says no and wants to study. Why are you forcing?
- We discussed this before, and don't want to go into arguments again and again. She can always study.
- It is not easy for a girl to continue study after getting engaged.
- Those days are gone, and times are changing. So many girls do it, and she can do it too. I propose that Tabassum meets Ashraf at least once, and she will change the mind. I will talk to them and arrange a meeting this Sunday. Tell her to be ready for it.
- Yes, I will tell—Zaheda had resigned on this issue.

On Sunday, the meeting arranged.

Tabassum decided to meet and tell that she does not want to marry now.

The family of Ashraf arrived at the scheduled time. The snacks, sweets, and coffee served.

During this time, Ashraf was busy looking at Tabassum as if he had never seen her before. The desire got intensified more and more.

- Taboo, please take Ashraf to room so that you two can talk and understand each other better. Zaheda finally broke the silence.

Tabassum got up from the seat, and Ashraf looked at his mother who encouraged him to go.

Once in the room

- You are sweet looking, and I am truly lucky to have a woman like you.
- Sorry I have not yet decided and listen to what I am saying
- What? I am told, it is finalised between parents and this meeting is just a formality.
- Yes, decided by parents but I am not happy. That is the reason I agreed to meet and tell.
- But Why? I am a decent person, rich and with social status.
- I respect that, but want to study and not ready for any engagement.
- What is there to study now? Get married and have amenities of life. My father is extremely rich, and no need to work. Enjoy the life.
- I need education to be a knowledgeable person and knowledge gives confidence and respect.
- What confidence and respect you are talking? My father is not educated, and has ten MBA's working for him. Madam it is always money, money and money only.
- You may be right, but I am not money minded and money has no significant importance in life.
- What is then essential in life?
- It is love and affection.
- I can give that.
- But I can't—I don't love you.
- You don't love me?—Are you serious or making me angry. Madam I am a rough person. I get what I want in life. There are no two issues. I want you and will get you.

He started leaving the room and took time to compose.

Tabassum got terrified with his declared determination.

On entering the main room, he laughed.

- Mom, she is a very sweet girl. I am happy that you have the daughter-in-law you wanted.

Zaheda, nervous and confused.

Hameed was happy to hear that.

Tabassum did not come out of the room.

- Let's go. I have an urgent meeting. Invite them for a diner and then finalise the other things.

The Subedar family left.

Zaheda went to Tabassum's room, and found it locked.

She refused to open it.

- I don't want to meet you. You don't love me, and you don't care what your daughter wants, she shouted.

Hamid was angry and wanted to shout back, but Zaheda pacified him.

- We do love you. You are our only child. Please try to understand us. Zaheda muttered, standing near the door.

She could hear the sobbing Tabassum.

- This is non-sense, and I will not tolerate it. Hamid shouted back and went away.

The crying mother was standing near the door, requesting her to open it. Tabassum finally yielded and opened the door, ran into the soothing arms of her mother.

Ashraf was a disturbed and angry person.

He was hurt and had never faced this insulting situation.

He always got what he wanted.

She is refusing me . . . .

She is refusing me . . . .

She is refusing me . . . . The thought was haunting him.

She is talking of love . . . .

She is talking of love . . . .

She is talking of love . . . . Study is just an excuse . . . .

Is she in love with somebody?

If so I must find it out, he resolved.

He organised the sting operation which identified Iqbal as her lover . . .

He decided to meet Iqbal, find out the truth and then either threaten him or eliminate him from his sphere of life.

When Iqbal got the message that Ashraf wanted to meet him in his office, he was very eager and excited.

Iqbal wanted to convey the message to Tabassum, but it was impossible. Tabassum was house locked by Hamid. Finally, he took the help of Sakina to convey the message which he had received from Ashraf. Tabassum was worried as by now she had experienced a different perception of Ashraf which Iqbal was not aware.

She conveyed her worries and feelings to Iqbal through Sakina and made him aware of what had happened between them on that day. She had never used the name of Iqbal during that time and still Ashraf had located Iqbal. He was certainly a dangerous person.

Iqbal reached Ashraf's Office.

The office set up impressed him. The wealth displayed everywhere. Iqbal asked to sit in the reception. After half an hour the secretary took him to Ashraf's cabin.

-   Assalamo-Alaykum, Iqbal greeted Ashraf in the Muslim culture and extended the hand.

He did not respond to the greetings nor did he get up from his seat

-   Pease sit down and take that chair.
-   Iqbal looked at him and sat.
-   Listen to what I am saying, he commanded. I am getting married to Tabassum, and I have come to know that you have a love affair with her. I want to warn you and order you to get out of our life.
-   She is my childhood friend, we are not in love, and I am surprised that you have made this allegation. This is not true. She wants to continue her studies and is not ready for the marriage now.
-   I don't listen to this nonsense. Are you in love with her.?
-   Yes, I am in love with her as her friend. I want to help her as she had always done for me. I will request you to leave her and let her pursue the studies. I am sure with your status you can find the other girl.
-   I have not called you here to take advice and lessons. I love her, and I want to marry—this is final and if anyone comes in the way, I know how to handle. Mr. Iqbal, go now. This is a friendly warning. If you don't listen, then face the consequences and be responsible.

The secretary opened the door, and asked Iqbal to leave.

Iqbal was shocked, nervous and just left the office.

He was not sure how to inform Tabassum of the meeting and what happened.

CHAPTER 36

Amanullah called Hamid to office.

- We would like to finish the wedding within a week. You don't worry, I will manage everything, he said to Hamid.
- But what is the hurry. She is my only daughter, and I have to make proper arrangements.
- I told you that I will arrange everything, and you don't worry. Ashraf wants to get married, and I can't refuse.
- I cannot understand it. I must discuss with Zaheda and other family members.
- Yes, go and discuss but it has to be done.
- I can't understand this.
- Well, are you aware that your daughter has a lover? Ashraf called him to office, and that idiot threatened that he would run away. The name is Iqbal, and you know him. So go now and do as what I have said. Everything will be alright.
- Iqbal???—What!!!, the voice in high pitch. Ashraf had a meeting with Iqbal!!. Is that rascal planning to run away with my daughter? I will kill him.
- You don't have to kill him and get arrested. Get her married and we will take care of everything.

Hamid left office and rushed home. He wanted straight to go to Iqbal's house and fire his mother for what his son was planning and what he wanted to do. But he decided to take Zaheda with him and came home.

- There is good news. Amanullah wants the wedding to be done within a week. Ashraf is insisting on it. He is going to arrange everything, and we don't have to worry.
- How can we do it? And why so much hurry.
- Don't ask me the reason. Amanullah wants it, and we have to do it. Taboo has to get married and so what is wrong if we do it now.

Tabassum was listening to this and started crying.

- I don't want to get married now. Why don't you listen to me and leave me with my study?

She caught hold of Hamid's hand.

- Papa I beg you please don't destroy my life. I am your daughter and Allah has given you the responsibly to ensure that I am happily married. I don't like him.

Zaheda intervened.

- Please listen to her. Don't spoil her life. Why are you so adamant now? We love our daughter, and want her to be happy.

Hamid lost his temper.

- Do you want to know? You will be shocked to learn what your daughter is planning? She wants to run away with Iqbal. Ashraf has found it out. He had called Iqbal in his office and has warned him. Before our family name is damaged, the marriage has to be done. Amanullah is nice and worries for us. And we are idiots who want to help and think of our daughter, who is bent upon destroying her and our peaceful and respectable life. Look what Iqbal's aunty has done. She ran away. Iqbal will do the same thing. It is in family's blood.

Zaheda could not believe this.

Tabassum ran to her room.

She came out with a copy of Q'uran.

- Papa, you do believe in this holy book.
- What non-sense, he shouted, Go and keep Q'uran aside.
- No, you have no faith in me. I am telling you with this holy book in my hand that I am not going to do what you have been told. Iqbal is my childhood friend, I like him but never as my husband. But now because of this I have to think. I cannot marry Ashraf, and the intention is study. Running away with Iqbal is something I will never do. I love you both, and want to be your dutiful daughter. So please help me.

Zaheda caught hold of Hamid's hand.

- Please listen and believe her. She is still young, and marriage can wait. Let her finish the study and marry a man of her choice.
- You don't know my problems, my difficulties.

Hamid pulled up a chair and was shivering. The voice crumbled; he could not control and was in tears.

Zaheda ran near to him, Tabassum ran to get a glass of water.

- What is it Papa? Why are you so fearful? Please tell us your difficulties—we are one family—We are with you. Please tell us, Tabassum pleaded.

Hamid caught the hand of Zaheda and said,

- I am heavily in debt of Amanullah. It is a huge sum of Rs. 50 lakhs. He is forcing to give my daughter to his son.
- 50 lakhs!!! Zaheda voice was at the highest pitch. When did you get that money from him? Why? What did you with it? When was it?

Multiple questions—

Multiple worries—

Multiple heartbreaks—

- It was the biggest mistake of my life. He had tempted me with the lure of money, and I got trapped into his talk. It was the consignment of gold he wanted to bring from Dubai, and he wanted me to help him and offered good money. I agreed. You remember, I had gone out on a business trip, I had gone to Dubai. On return, Customs checked me at airport and confiscated the gold worth Rs. 50 Lacs. I was arrested. Amanullah had contacts with the customs and police and arranged the release from jail. He replaced me in jail with other person. I don't know how he managed. Since that date, I am under his obligations. I pleaded with him to relieve me, and he agreed as I was not the person needed for that work. He threatened me not to tell this to anyone and took away my passport.
- I was relieved, and our life went on as usual. It seems Ashraf saw Tabassum one day somewhere and wanted to marry her. Amanullah called me and gave the proposal. I refused and went on refusing because of his business activities. He had acquired strong social status, and respect, but people hardly knew the real status. Finally, he threatened me that if I don't make his son happy by giving my daughter, he will go to the police get me arrested. I am afraid he will carry out his threat and make our life miserable.

There was pin drop silence in the room.

- Zaheda's sobbing had turned into crying.
- Hamid could not lift his face and meet the eyes of his wife and daughter. He prayed to Allah to take his life now so that the agonies of the family are resolved. With his folded hand, covered the face, and prayed.
- Papa, don't worry, Tabassum finally broke the silence.
- I am ready to marry him, and you go ahead with the marriage. I am your daughter and Allah has ordained that I obey you. My Jannat is under the feet of my mother, and I cannot ruin her life. My only request is call Iqbal. I want to talk to him.

Zaheda was stunned

Hamid was shocked

Tabassum ran to the room holding the Q'uran in hand.

She knew what she committed was while holding the Q'uran in hand.

A daughter had fulfilled her obligations of life.

CHAPTER 37

On reaching home Sharifa looked at Iqbal and realised something has gone wrong

- What has happened? Why your face is so worried and gloomy.
- Nothing mom, I am disturbed by what has happened and how much sufferings you are facing. We have no news of him and Shabana. I honestly don't know what is happening in our life.
- Keep faith in Allah, he is testing our suffering strength and will solve our problems. Nanaji wants to take us and is advising that it will help.
- I think he is right, and we should listen to him.
- But what happens if Abdullah comes back? What will he do and where will he go?.
- Don't worry. He did not worry and left us in this condition.
- You should not talk like this. We don't know what happened and what made him do this.
- I am sorry mom; let us plan what to do next. We will leave a message here that we are with Nana, and he should come there.
- OK do as you wish.

Masood and Shirin had gone out. Iqbal just went to his room and started to think how to solve Tabassum's problem. He planned to run away with her, but the sheer thought of mother's pain and agony did not allow him to continue.

He was now convinced that Ashraf was not a good person, and he had to find a way to help her. He had no solution and heard mother's voice asking to come out and talk to Nana. He looked at watch; an hour had passed in thoughts of Tabassum.

- We decided to go to our place for few days. This will give you change of atmosphere and rest, Masood said.

Shirin joined and supported Masood.

Sharifa agreed and decided to leave after Friday's prayers.

There was a knock at the door. Iqbal opened the door, and Himmatlal was there.

- Do you know where those idiots are? Where they are hiding?
- No, we have no idea. Masood said
- Those idiots, ran away to Dubai. How? Who helped them?? Read this letter of Hasmukh.
- Iqbal took the letter and read it.
- Yes, indeed in Dubai and are happy. Hasmukh asked for forgiveness.
- My forgiveness?? Yes, never, never he gets it. I think your father has run away with them. I am still wondering how they went, Hasmukh had no passport. Did Shabana had a passport??
- No, she had no passport, Iqbal asserted.
- Then how it can happen. I just came to inform you and find out if Shabana wrote any letter to you. I will now go to Police and report the matter. Police will help to get them back here. I am not going to leave them in peace—your daughter and husband made my life miserable.

After he left, Iqbal said,

- Nana, how can he be sure that the letter was from Dubai? Has he seen the postmark on the envelope? It must be the trick to mislead him so that he does not look for them.
- You may be right my son, but let us not worry. If Shabana is happy with him—let them be happy. We have only two days left to finish other important work.

Yes, he indeed had an urgent work to do. How to meet Tabassum and needed Sakina's help. He did not hear the knock at the door. He did not hear the voice of his mother.

- Tabassum and Zaheda are here, Iqbal come out, Sharifa shouted.

He just did not believe, and looked at Tabassum. She was not what used to be. The smile on face had vanished. The mischief in eyes missing.

Shirin welcomed them.

- I came to give you good news. Tabassum is getting married next week as her in-laws want the marriage to be performed because Ashraf has to leave for business and will be away for a long time.

Iqbal was silent and stunned.

- This is something good. But why so much hurry, Sharifa asked
- Yes, but Amanullah is insisting. We cannot help it. I came on the request of Tabassum to inform and invite. There is no time to print and distribute the invitation cards, and we decided to invite only close relatives and friends.
- We are planning to leave from here on Friday. You are aware what happened in the family. Sharifa needs a change, Shirin intervened.
- Yes, Go Away, Tabassum spoke in high pitch, caught hold of Iqbal's hand and dragged him to his room.
- What are you doing this—getting married? What about studies? Iqbal asked in the low tone.
- My destiny Iqbal—my dreams are shattered, but I have to fulfil a duty in life. I cannot tell you more. Do not ask me. I don't want you to be there. You please go away somewhere. I don't want you to attend the marriage.
- You are not happy, then why?

I cannot tell you. It is the destiny, and Allah's wish. You go away, and don't be there. She ran and went out.

Zaheda knew the agony of her daughter but was helpless.

Sharifa walked in with glasses of Sherbet. Zaheda first refused. Sharifa came with the glass to Tabassum and gave the glass in her hand. Holding the hand of Sharifa, Tabassum drank the sherbet. Sharifa sensed a feeling of discomfort, pain and agony but could not understand it. Tabassum hugged her, controlled her emotions, bade goodbye and walked out of the door.

For Iqbal, the dream had ended.

It was for the first time Sharifa realised what she had not understood.

Was Iqbal in love with her?

Was Tabassum in love with Iqbal?

Why she never think of it . . . Why?

CHAPTER 38

The tormented Iqbal had sleepless night. Masood and Shirin occupied his room so he was with the mother. The sleepless night was felt by Sharifa.

- Why you are not sleeping, Sharifa asked.
- Yes, mom, I am not getting sleep. You please sleep and don't worry.
- Can I not worry? Why you did not tell me earlier.
- What mom?
- Tabassum—I could see in her eyes the love for you. I never realised that you loved her.
- How can you tell?
- I am a woman, I sensed it, I am your mother, and I feel the pain of it.
- Mom why she decided to marry a rascal like Ashraf. She wanted to study and be a doctor.—Why Mom? Why?
- There has to be a strong reason for it. I don't know what it is, but she is giving a sacrifice. When a daughter does this. It must be for the family. It must be for the father. I honestly don't know what it is, but it is done and you cannot stop it.
- I can mom, tomorrow I go get hold of her hand and bring her here. You arrange a Kazi, and our Nikah. She will be my wife and then her miseries of life will be over.
- No, my son, her miseries of life will begin. The miseries of your life will begin. Never think of an act against the dictates of Allah.
- Then why Allah is doing this to her.?
- I am not enlightened enough to tell you that—but lessons of my life thought me that HE has reason. HE knows everything. You must have courage and faith in HIM.

- I will pray for you. She got up as it was time for her midnight prayers.—will you pray with me? Allah loves midnight prayers.
- Yes, Mom, I will, I need peace in my mind. My mind is full of anger and revenge.

Sharifa and Iqbal got up for the prayers.

After the prayers, Sharifa went to Iqbal who was on the bed. She took his head on her lap . . . When she had done this last was not in her memory, but years must have passed. Iqbal felt the soothing hand of mother on head and slipped into the cradle of sleep.

Next day morning, Iqbal thought of going to Tabassum's house. He was keen to tell her what Ashraf had said and how dangerous man he is. He wanted to tell her of the proposal of getting married at once so that the complications will end soon.

He wanted a reason to go there. He found one.

He bought a bouquet and gift for her and went.

Hamid opened the door and saw him with the bouquet and the gift box.

- What is this and why are you here?
- Uncle, we yesterday got intimation of Tabassum marriage. As we are leaving and not able to attend marriage, I thought to give my gift to her.

Zaheda had reached the door and saw Iqbal talking to Hamid.

- We have decided not to accept any gift for the marriage. So thank you very much and you can take it back; your prayers and blessings are what we need so please pray for her happiness. Zaheda said.
- Yes, indeed, Hamid joined her.

Tabassum came running pushed her parents aside and closed the door.

- Iqbal go away and leave me alone, she shouted.

Dejected Iqbal stood there for few seconds. He decided to leave the flowers and gift at the door. He removed the private letter which he had hidden in the perfume bottle. While leaving the flowers, he could not stop the tears from eyes.

Was he laying the flowers on the grave of his childhood friend?

The tears ran faster.

He walked dejected without looking back.

The day finally arrived.

Iqbal left Mumbai with Sharifa.

CHAPTER 39

Amanullah asked Hamid to meet.

- I hope you have had a talk with your family. Are you sure that she is not going to run away from the house?
- Please respect my child, now she is even a part of your family. She agreed for the marriage giving due respect to parents wish.
- It is good to hear that. Now listen, we have finalised this Sunday as the wedding reception day. The Nikah will be in the main hall and the reception in our spacious community hall.
- There is hardly four days left, and we are not prepared yet, Hamid intervened.
- You don't have to do. Let your wife. What is her name?
- Zaheda
- Yes, I remember now. Ask her to meet my wife, and she will give her ornaments, dresses etc, which you will give it to your daughter. She will give you even the things which you would give to your son-in-law. You don't have to spend a rupee. This is arranged, and anyhow everything is going to come back to us only, he said sarcastically.
- I certainly don't like this and need time. We are a respectable family and wish to do things as per social customs—please understand this, Hamid pleaded
- Yes, I know your respects, and I don't have time. Give me the list of people whom you want to invite, and the cards will be sent to them. Everything is arranged by my son. You must thank Allah that you have an intelligent son-in-law, he said laughingly.

- Yes, Indeed, Allah has blessed me.
- Make sure that she does not run away. I have kept watch dogs, and warning you. If she runs away, they both will be shot dead.
- Hamid felt like getting buried in the ground, He left and walked back.

On reaching home, he spoke to Zaheda and made her familiar with the demands and commands of Amanullah.

There was hardly any time. They decided that they would not invite any friends in the marriage. Only the first relatives and would meet them and explain the urgency of the situation.

Zaheda listed out her jewelleries and decided to give everything to Tabassum. She had no desire now for any jewellery and had decided to be away from the social events and social life.

She took out the wedding sari and looked at it. The sheer thought of her wedding night thrilled her. With sari in her one hand, she looked at Hamid. Hamid looked at it but could not realise the intent. What was happening to Tabassum had totally disheartened him

Zaheda expressed the desire that let Tabassum wear the same wedding sari which she had worn.

- I don't know whether they will like it. It is an old sari, and it is possible that they might give a dress for her to wear it, Hamid replied.
- I will request them and make them agree, Zaheda said.
- When you will go to meet Ashraf's mother.
- Should I take Tabassum with me?
- No, I don't think so.—Go alone and meet them.

Tabassum had gone out with Sakina. Iqbal had left a week ago, and the void was difficult to fill. She had no contact of him and was even regretting the way she closed the door on him.

- What else could I have done? She asked Sakina.
- I understand your pain, but you should have controlled yourself. Why did you agree for this marriage?
- I cannot and will not discuss this with anyone. It is my destiny.
- Will you make him happy? Will you be happy?

- I don't think so, but now I am not looking at happiness. I now look at sufferings and want to prepare myself for it.
- How can you prepare yourself for sufferings?
- There are many ways—I have learnt from Sharifa Aunty. Since the day I have started understanding the meaning of life, I have watched her. Her sufferings of a lousy husband are not seen by you. I have seen but not understood. The strongest was her prayers. I will be now punctual for my daily prayers. I will ask Allah, why HE blessed me with this pain. HE has HIS own reason and only through my prayers I will get the answer. You will see it Sakina—One day, you will see it.

She lost control of her emotions and was in tears, but she wiped it out quickly.

- I am sorry; I lost control on my emotions. I will suffer but will not cry. This is what I have learnt from Sharifa aunt, and I am going to practice it, practice it and practice it.
- You are a changed Tabassum—you are totally changed. I can only pray that you get your mischievous smile back. I am always there for you. Let's go now.

On reaching home, Zaheda informed of the marriage date and how the wedding organised.

- Mom, I am ready and went away.

The four days passed, and Sunday arrived.

Morning hours were busy.

As per the traditions of Nikah, two witnesses approached Tabassum and asked if she agreed to her Nikah with Ashraf and permitted her father to do the religious Ceremony on her behalf.

She said, "Qabool Hai"—I agree as required by the religious rules.

The Nikah ceremony performed in the hall. Mostly members of Amanullah's family and friends were present. Hamid's brother from Hyderabad attended the marriage.

Lunch served was fabulous, and the invitees had a delicious taste of it.

The Reception in the evening was attended by a large group of business people. The decoration was excellent reflecting the wealth of Amanullah.

Tabassum dressed in a dark green sari, and worn diamond jewelleries. Ashraf was in a golden sherwani and a matching head gear.

Tabassum's dazzling beauty was a topic of the young boys and girls attending the function. Few commented on the luck of Ashraf to get a beautiful wife. Many wondered why Tabassum selected an ugly looking man as husband. Few joked that money is a big source of love and it was money, money and money to have an ultra comfortable life. What else does a woman want?

Amanullah was busy meeting dignitaries, important socialites, police officers and government officials. They were praising the excellent wedding arrangements. Guests greeted the bride and groom. Photographs shot in plenty.

During these formalities Tabassum was silent and the face expressionless. The handshakes were like shaking of a dead body. The warmth, the feelings, the sensual touch were gone.

Ashraf noticed the coldness, aloofness and was missing the mischievous smile. Tabassum's face, the glare of eyes, and fragrance of sexuality had attracted him when he had seen her for the first time and decided to marry her. These were missing and many times he reminded her to be active.

Now was the time to take the bride home.

They both headed for the car. A brand new Merc presented by Ashraf to Tabassum. The Merc, decorated tastefully was envied by the guests.

Before leaving the reception hall, Tabassum had to meet parents. Hamid and Zaheda came near. Hamid could not look into the eyes of his daughter. Zaheda embraced her as if she was a five year old child in her arms. Tears were unstoppable. Tabassum had no expressions. Family members separated them and lead Tabassum to the car.

At home, the wedding cake cutting formality celebrated. One of the finest and expensive cake was on display. "Tabassum weds Ashraf" written with golden coins of 1 gm. The cake cut and distributed; the lucky ones got the coins along with the slice of cake. Loud music was on, and the atmosphere created to the liking of Ashraf, by Ashraf and for Ashraf.

Tabassum was led to wedding room by Ashraf's sister Abeda. Inside the room, the fragrance of Jasmine was intoxicating. The blooming flowers and the decorated room stunned Abeda. She never had known the taste of Ashraf; as she hardly ever reacted with the arrogant brother. She looked at Tabassum and gave a mischievous smile. Tabassum was silent. Abeda wanted to have good fun with her, tease her, torment her and had even created stories of Ashraf to be told. But the coldness of Tabassum spoiled the mood and intentions.

Two glasses of Milk prepared in the rusk of almonds kept on the table.

- Now wait for Ashraf to come and enjoy, she said, and closed the door and went away.

After cutting the cake, Ashraf was dragged out by his friends to have a final drink session.

Tabassum was alone sitting on the bed. The thought of Iqbal was lingering on and on, but she controlled not to indulge further, being married. Prayer was the only solution and she started praying.

She was in her prayers and the door opened with a bang. Ashraf could not believe what he saw.

- You are praying at this time! Are you mad? This is our wedding night. Get up from your prayers, I need you.

He was drunk. He wanted the wife. He wanted to snatch her, drag her but could not do it, as if someone protected her.

Tabassum finished her prayer and was standing near the chair.

Ashraf pulled her to bed. Tabassum closed her eyes. Her senses had died. She was not feeling what Ashraf was doing to her. Ashraf could not bear this and wanted her to react. The response was not coming.

Ashraf satisfied his physical needs.

A wife was raped by her husband.

CHAPTER 40

Masood on reaching home wanted the guidance and advice for the job of Iqbal. He had realised the pain of Iqbal though he was not confident and never wanted to discuss the issue with Sharifa. Shirin was of the same opinion, and decided to concentrate more on the future.

Hussain came to meet and talked to Sharifa and Iqbal. He had the sympathies for what had happened and recommended that Iqbal goes to Calcutta to work with his friend Karimbhai who has a growing business and looking for a reliable person.

- He is a matured and reliable person needs a young man for the office and I recommended your name, he told Iqbal.
- But uncle I don't want to be separated from mother. I would like to be near her., Iqbal replied.
- It may not be possible but later on you may call her there and she will be with you. She is with her father and not alone, so you don't worry.
- Yes, Sure, she will be with her father, but I will be without my mother.
- I understand and appreciate the sentiments—but life has to go on. This is an excellent opportunity, and I don't like that you miss it.
- I agree, Masood said.

Shirin walked with the cup of tea.

- Where is Sharifa, please call her.
- She is in the kitchen cooking and will need time there.
- You go and send her here, we need her.

Shirin went and sent Sharifa

- Hussainbhai has decent offer for Iqbal, but he has to go to Calcutta. Iqbal wants your consent and is not willing to go without you.

Sharifa looked at Iqbal.

She could truly feel the fear and worries of Iqbal.

- Don't worry Iqbal. I will be most happy. You go and start your life. I want my son to achieve something in life.
- I will fulfil your wish and go mom, Iqbal spoke and hug Sharifa.

So it was finalised.

Iqbal left for Calcutta.

Karimbhai's PA Mansoor received Iqbal at the station. He was taken to the quarters where other staffs were staying. He shared room with Chunilal, a middle aged man working in shipping, logistics of the business.

- Rest for a day here and Karimseth will see you in the office to-morrow, Mansoor said.

There is the staff canteen, and you will get what you need there. Chunilal will explain you and take you there once he is here. Mansoor left, and Iqbal was alone in the room.

Taher from the other room walked and introduced himself as a Salesman working with the company since last three years. He was from Mumbai and happy with the company. Iqbal made friends with him and got more information which he needed. On hearing that Taher was sharing room with three more employees, he dropped the idea of asking if he can move with him. In this room, he was alone with Chunilal who was senior to him.

He ate in the canteen with Taher and had formal hand shake with other staff. He was tired and wanted to rest, but desired to call Sharifa. Taher took him to the nearby telephone booth and he called Sharifa.

Next day morning, he was in the office where the secretary made him wait in the reception as Karimseth was busy in the meeting.

He learned the first lesson of the commercial life. Though the office timings were at 10 AM, Karimseth used to be in office by 8-30 and dealt other business and pending issues without the help of any assistant. He understood the demands of his business and how to execute.

Karimseth called Iqbal to his office.

- So you are Iqbal, Hussain told me and has given an extremely good reference, he said. Sit down and tell me what you wish to say.
- Iqbal gave full details of educational life and wanted to show the certificates.

- I don't like these certificates. I am interested in your life, not your education.

Iqbal was nervous.

Does he know about my father?

Does he know about aunty Shabana?

Does he know about Tabassum?

- I am just beginning my working life. The education had priority, and I had a contended life. My parents gave the required religious training, and are a strong believer in Allah.
- That is not new, every true Muslim has to be a devotee of Allah, else is not a Muslim. What in social life? Have you done any significant work to help someone?
- No, I never had any opportunity or occasion except help colleagues in the study.
- Good, but remember my son, what you learn in schools, colleges is knowledge. What you don't learn is the application of this knowledge. I have not even completed my preliminary school education. I had to work to support my parents. My experience and my social connections brought me what I am now. So keep this in mind. If you want happiness, make sure that you make others happy.

This was the second lesson which Iqbal had learnt today.

- You will be working with Chunilal; he is hard working and knows the business well. I will keep a watch on your work and performance. I like you and want you to be something.

Chunilal came, and Iqbal was handed over to him.

- Wait, you did not ask your salary, Karimseth said.
- You pay only after seeing the work. I have faith in my abilities, and faith in your judgement.
- But still tell me—you have to take care of the parents. By the way, what the father is doing?

This was a shock to Iqbal—Is he testing me? Iqbal was not sure.

- Sir, this is a painful part of my life, and I would not want to bring this into my working life. I need your respect. Can I tell you after you evaluated my performance?
- Ok, I respect your feelings. Chunilal, take this young man into your custody and teach him the business.

Iqbal went with Chunilal and Karimseth observing Iqbal's walk.

A straight walk with firm steps and high head.

He felt this is the boy who will achieve, if trained properly.

Iqbal's working days started.

Next day morning he was in the office at 8-30. When Karimseth walked in, he saw Iqbal working at the desk.

- What are you doing now so early? Office timings are from 10.
- Sir I have learnt two lessons yesterday. First do not work like a clock. It goes round and round.
- And the other one? Karimseth could not hold his inquisitiveness.
- If you want to be happy—make others happy. And I want you to be happy, Iqbal said.
- May Allah bless you—you indeed have learnt fast and he walked into his office.

Six months passed. Karimseth did not call Iqbal even once, but kept an eye on performance, Chunilal reporting on Iqbal's activities.

So now tell me what salary do you want?

- Sir, if I had to tell the salary, I would have told on the first day.
- Yes, I remember it. But still you have to tell me.
- I will never say it and will accept whatever you give. My only request is to give me a week's holiday so that I can visit my mother.
- Why, call her here.
- Where will I keep her? I cannot afford a house still to keep her.
- Who says you don't have a house. From today, you are promoted as manager export and you will manage the exports to Africa and Europe. The company will give you the house and you happily stay with mother. This is what I decided. Are you happy?—The salary is still a secret, and will be disclosed when you open the envelop.

Iqbal could not believe it.

Has Allah answered her mother's prayers?

In a stroke of emotion, he caught hold of Karimseth's hand and with respect and compassion, he did his salutations.

Karimseth had no son who can do this salutation. He embraced Iqbal.

- Go and meet your mother. Bring her here, the house will be ready, and I would like to meet her. Hussain has told me the tragedy of her life and I want to meet this strong lady. Go my son, Go.

Iqbal called Sharifa and gave the happy news, spoke with Masood and told that he is coming back for a week to meet and then take Sharifa with him.

- I am flying back home. I will be picked up at the airport by a car and will drive from there to the village, Iqbal told Masood.
- No, we are coming to the airport and then we will come together. Sharifa wants to go to home. It is possible Abdullah might have written a letter. The house needs to be cleaned. We will see you at the airport—Masood told.
- Sharifa just could not control the emotions over the phone. She was in tears. Come soon Iqbal, Come soon, this is what she only could utter.

This was Iqbal's first ever travelling by air. The life had indeed changed.

He opened the envelop. There was a cheque of Rs. 50000/-, the salary of last six months and an appointment letter promoting him to be Manager of Export division. Salary of Rs. 15000/—plus the perks—a furnished company house and a company car.

He performed his Sajada and thanked Allah.

He was flying high.

For a moment, he thought of Tabassum. Is she married by now?—Is she happy?? He had no news of her since last seven months. He prayed that she did not marry. He can go to Hamid and ask Tabassum's hand in marriage. He had everything that Hamid wanted for his daughter.

CHAPTER 41

Iqbal landed at Bombay Airport.

Sharifa and Masood arrived to receive him. The thrill and excitement of seeing Iqbal was visible on her face.

Finally, Iqbal came out. Sharifa could not recognise him. Iqbal saw her and came running to hug her. He lifted her and in the excitement forgot that he was at the airport, and people were watching.

A suited man was not Sharifa's vision of Iqbal.

Iqbal put her on the ground, took her right hand and did the salutation, the way he was taught.

Masood watched this and finally joined them. Iqbal paid respect in the traditional way.

Iqbal saw a man holding a board with his name displayed. He was from the Car Rental Services, after taking charge of the luggage and arranging the things he inquired where he has to go. Masood directed him to the house. The driver was bit shocked. He had a different image and picture of the man he was picking from the airport as given to him by the boss. The place where asked to go was not even in his dream. He looked twice at Iqbal and could not find the answer to his inquisitiveness.

During the journey Sharifa was just holding Iqbal's hand, and had no questions to ask. The prayers answered by Allah and she had no further questions. She was listening to what Iqbal was saying to Masood. The experiences, new demands of life, the boss Karimseth, colleague Chunilal, who taught him everything about the business were narrated by Iqbal with clear concept. The talk continued and Sharifa listened peacefully.

Iqbal reached home. The narrow street, old building and the conversations heard during the journey resolved the inquisitiveness of the driver. He developed affection for Iqbal and remembered his son who was struggling in life. Can he get a break in life like Iqbal?

After dropping him, he asked Iqbal

- Sir, I was told that I have to drop you to Nasik and be with you as long as you need me.
- Yes you are right—but this is my house—I stay here for a day or two and then go to Nasik. So be with me.
- Sir, I will be in the car and you call me when needed.

Sharifa had cleaned the house before one day and knew what her son expected.

Iqbal learnt about Husain's ill health and was keen to go to Nasik.

He was equally keen to meet Hamid and make him aware of his progress and new status in life.

He wanted to meet Tabassum.

- Yes, she married the week after you left. Hamid was in hurry and did not invite any friends and relatives in the wedding. We were not here and cannot tell you much, Sharifa briefed him on Tabassum.

Iqbal met Sakina.

- Any news from her?, Iqbal asked.
- No—not even once she talked to me after she left.
- Are you sure she is happy? Is there any way I can meet her.
- No, I doubt. She stays far away in bungalow at Versova somewhere near the beach. I am not aware where it is.
- Where is her husband's office—what was his name, I forgot.
- Ashraf, and the office is somewhere in Worli. I can take you there as I had gone once with Tabassum. I can't tell the name of the office and where it is in the building. It is a big building, we were standing on the road, Ashraf came and Tabassum went in the car. I stood there just wondering, thinking, dreaming and fearing.
- What was there to fear?
- Tabassum never wanted this. She was simple, she wanted to study, and achieve something different. The dreams were shattered.
- I will find it out and if needed you take me to the office.
- Yes I will.

Iqbal was thinking how to resolve this issue. New learning of life had taught him the new mantra—"Never Accept No As An Answer"

On reaching home, Masood learnt that Hussain was not well and wanted to go back. Hussain had played a major role in the life of Iqbal. Iqbal never wanted to be away when needed, and decided to leave. Tabassum can wait.

Hussain had suffered a chest-pain and diagnosed with blockages. Doctors gave the opinion for the operation but he was not ready and willing to go for it. Doctor advised complete bed rest for a month and review and see the effect of medicine.

Iqbal was running short of time. He had taken a leave for a week only. He had to still do the final packing as he was planning to take Sharifa with him. He had to meet Tabassum and resolve the issues. He was confused and wanted to extend the leave. His mind did not accept the thought of extension. It would be inappropriate, and he never wanted to create a bad impression. He had no genuine reason which can convince Karimseth who was strict in business discipline.

He finally decided to go back and come back again if required.

Hussain came home.

He knew the progress of Iqbal as he was in constant touch with Karimseth but he never disclosed this to anyone.

He knew Allah was rewarding the wish of his deceased sister Maimuna,

He knew Allah had answered the prayers of Sharifa.

He knew Iqbal was on the right track and had a good future.

He knew Karimseth had a daughter and he was thinking of Iqbal as his family member, as his son-in-law.

Finally the day came and Iqbal left back for Calcutta with Sharifa. Flying was a new experience for Sharifa.

On reaching Calcutta, the car picked them from the airport. This was his car and the driver. On reaching home, he could not believe that he was now going to live in a big spacious flat furnished with taste and dignity, there were two house servants appointed. Sharifa was in utter disbelief, sat on the sofa and asked for a glass of water.

Iqbal called Karimseth.

- Sir, I am grateful to Allah for making me as your servant. You have given me so much happiness. I can't express the same.
- Don't mention, you are getting what you deserve. How is your mother? Is she with you now? I would like to meet her.
- You can talk to her now.
- No, No I will meet her personally first. Tell me when I can come to your house.

- It is your house you can come at any time.
- OK then I will see you at 5 PM. Take rest and hope everything is ok, if you need anything just inform.
- Yes I do, but the house is perfect.
- Yes it is arranged by my daughter, Hasina. She will be with me in the evening. See you then.

This was a shock to Iqbal.

He knew nothing about Karimseth's family.

He knew nothing about Hasina.

CHAPTER 42

Tabassum's life had totally changed. She was engaged in prayers and spiritual duties. She did not meet other family members, except at lunch and dinner time, normal smiles, and routine show of love and affection.

Ashraf used to be hardly present during those hours. His drunken late comings were a daily ritual. Tabassum just used to surrender her body to him, and he used to satisfy his desires. The intimacy of a woman was missing which he hardly realised in drunken state.

Tabassum had totally cut off her social life. Zaheda sometimes tried to call her and talk. The responses and conversations were lifeless. Mother realised the agony of daughter. Hamid had no strength even to phone and talk. He was suffering the agony of life.

One day Amanullah called Hamid to his office.

- How are you? He greeted him and ordered coffee for them.
- I am fine, and life is going on as usual.
- Tabassum is extremely happy in our house, and she gets the required comforts, I hope you are aware.
- Yes, indeed we are aware of and are grateful to Ashraf for taking loving care of her.
- Now see I need your help and want you to do a small favour to me.
- I do, if I can. I don't want to get involved in any of your business activity. I cannot meet that need.
- Yes, I made that mistake once, and you made me suffer a loss of 50 lakhs, which you had said you will pay me back. Not a rupee has been paid by you.

- Yes, I was stressed and wanted to get out of jail. I just said under stress, but can never repay. The business risk was yours.
- But you gave me in writing. I have that letter with me with your passport. Forget the past, this time is easy. You don't have to do anything. You don't have to go out.
- What is it then?
- You have to keep one suitcase in your house for a week.
- Why in my house when you have a spacious house? What is in the suitcase—gold again?
- No money in gold now. Those days are over. The drugs are now money making business.
- No, please don't drag me into this. My wife will not agree.
- Make her understand—it is your responsibility. She is your wife, and she has to obey you. The women in our family don't questions us, and do what is asked. This is man's world. Do you understand this simple statement?
- No, I will not. You find someone else.
- This is not polite of you. No one will even suspect. and just a matter of may be eight days.
- This is not possible without my wife knowing, and I don't want to get her involved. Please try to understand my situation.
- She will not even know. What I plan is that you both go out of Mumbai and my man will come and keep the suitcase in your house. My man will visit and you introduce her as your friend. He will look at your house and decide where to hide the bag.
- Now that is not possible. She knows my friends and this new friend will create suspicion. I honestly don't want to do.
- I will give you hundred thousand—one lac for keeping the bag for a week. You can buy a diamond necklace. She will be truly happy. There is no problem, and you don't have to think further.

The thought of one lac weakened him.

- But what will happen if the bag is found out in my house?

The voice changed, and Amanullah knew he had hit the weak spot.

- No one will even know. Ok I will give two laces, so that you can give a diamond necklace to your daughter. So final and done.
- Are you sure? This is safe, and nothing will happen to me. Today evening I will take her out and then let first your man see the house and we will decide after that.

- You are a genius, and we do it so. Enjoy your evening and give me your house key. My man will come and inspect.

Hameed gave the key and left the office.

- On the way, he was thinking.
- This is safe and secure and only for a week.
- He had not given a gift to Zaheda since long.
- Two diamond necklaces—an unfulfilled dream.

CHAPTER 43

Zaheda was bit surprised by the offer of Hamid to go out for a movie. She had not been with him since a long time and remembered earlier days when they were not missing any movie. Life after Tabassum's marriage was extremely dull, and agreed to the opportunity. After the movie, they went out for dinner and returned home late.

On reaching home, Zaheda realised that something had gone wrong in the house. How can it happen? She noticed that the pillows on the bed were not in the original location. Hamid used hard pillows, and she used soft pillows. The hard pillows used to be always on the left side of the bed. Today it was not the same. It has never happened in 25 years of their married life.

- Hamid, something is wrong. Our pillows are exchanged. The bedspread is not my usual style. I can't figure out what has happened.
- What Zaheda, you are sometimes extremely funny and confusing. You must have forgotten and by mistake kept it.

Hamid was nervous but controlled himself. He knew Amanullah cheated and had put the bag in the house.

- No, I am sure. I had my afternoon nap before you came and my pillow was on my side
- Please don't worry and make an issue. You must have forgotten, now it is too late, and let us go to sleep.

A worried Zaheda had no other choice.

Hamid knew the bag was under the bed.

Next day he went to Amanullah's office to verify his conclusion. He was right. Amanullah apologised saying it was urgent and he had to do it. Hamid never discussed the suspicion of Zaheda. He wanted to ask Amanullah to give the pledged money, but could not muster enough courage to do so.

He came back, and while walking was dreaming of his two diamond necklaces. He thought, they will go to the jeweller and see what she likes.

He entered the house, and Sakina was there.

- See what she is saying?
- What?—A shocked Hamid could not believe it.
- She had come to our house. She knocked the door, and nobody opened it.
- How someone will open it when we were out?
- That is the issue. She says there was no lock on the door which you put when we are out of the house. On not seeing the lock, she rang the bell, and there was no answer. Did you not put the extra lock on the door which you always do when we go out?
- Oh that, I had honestly forgotten about it. We were in a hurry, and it just escaped my mind. See everything in the house is Ok. Nobody came, and nothing is stolen from our house. I think we are getting older. I forgot to put the lock, and you forgot to put the pillows in the right order.

A confused Zaheda had no answer. But in her own mind she knew something has gone wrong.

Two days passed, nothing happened, and she got adjusted to her daily routines.

Hamid again went to Amanullah's Office and was informed that they had gone out and expected after two days.

Two days later there was a raid on Amanullah's office and home.

A group of Police officers were at both the places with permission to search the places. They found incriminating documents in the office. The office sealed and closed. The officers did not find anything in the house, but the raid created a talk of the town and people were gossiping. This made life of the family members difficult, and they locked themselves in the house.

There was no trace of Amanullah and Ashraf.

Hamid and Zaheda were stressed, but had no way of helping their daughter. Tabassum was not interested in the event and kept at a distance.

Next day morning there were news of police encounter and the shooting of three gangsters. By the after-noon, it was identified and confirmed that Amanullah and Ashraf were shot dead.

The office was sealed and taken over by the authorities. The investigation exposed a massive drug operation being carried out by them in association with the politicians. The feud between two politicians had created this information leak, and confiscation of a large consignment. Politicians planned elimination of Amanullah and Ashraf to save their public disgrace.

Hamid was a troubled man.
His dream of diamond necklace shattered.
The thought of a suitcase lying in the house tormented him.

Chapter 44

Karimseth and Hasina came on the scheduled time.

Iqbal and Sharifa met them at the door and welcomed them.

Karimseth said to Sharifa

- I am happy to meet you. Iqbal is talented and hardworking.
- It is Allah's blessing, Sharifa replied.
- Yes, it is always, but a mother plays a significant role, and you have been an excellent mother. I have learnt lot about you from Hussain. This is my daughter Hasina.

Hasina greeted her, and Sharifa blessed her with a kiss on the forehead.

- She is doing the interior designing, and she has done what you see in this house. I hope you like it.
- Yes, indeed it is remarkably well done, Iqbal said and looked at her.

The eyes met for the first time. She smiled and then looked again at Sharifa.

- I will go and make tea for you, Sharifa said
- Why you have to go, the servant is there, and he will make it.
- No, servants are meant to assist and help me. The guests are mine, and I serve.

Karimseth impressed by the creative thinking and her humility.

- Iqbal you have to take care of Hasina and teach her the ethics of running a business. She wants to open her own interior designing business. She is skilled in designing but running a business, she is blank and a novice
- What can I teach her, she is knowledgeable and intelligent; Iqbal said and looked at her?

This time she focussed on him. The stunning eyes made him nervous, and he shifted to face Karimseth.

- Business has its own ethics and rules. These things are learned from your own experience and associations of life. She is not exposed to that part of business, and I like that she works with you for this time, learns the ethics and then start her own business. I hope you don't object in your busy work schedule.
- No, certainly not, but I am learning so much from you.

Iqbal looked at her. She focussed on him, but now the eyes had a mischievous look. The nervousness increased.

Sharifa walked with the tray, and Iqbal served them. While giving Hasina her cup, he touched her hand and the smoothness of skin made him more nervous.

- You certainly make an excellent tea. I have not enjoyed tea like this. Are you using different flavour? Karimseth inquired.
- Yes, it is which I have learned from my mother. I don't have a daughter so I will teach it to Iqbal's wife when time comes, she said and laughed.
- You can teach Hasina, he said without realising the gist of it.
- Yes, I can teach her, she is my daughter now. Do you enjoy working in the kitchen? She asked Hasina.
- Not very much Aunty, I hate kitchen, I have never been to the kitchen, and there was never a need for it. But now with this tea, I have missed something.
- So now every day you come here in the morning, and I will teach you the tricks of the kitchen.
- From tomorrow I am going to work with Iqbal and start learning the ethics of business as wished by my father,
- That is something new for me. Iqbal never told me about it. It is reasonable than kitchen can wait.
- Mom this was decided now. Karimseth wants me to teach her and then she wants to continue her own business of interior designing. You know she had done this work in our house, and she is proficient at it.
- Yes, this is good—teach her well then.

Hasina left, and now Iqbal was wondering. Is she beautiful?

The inner voice confirmed . . .

- Iqbal tell me something about your business, Sharifa asked.

- Mom it is extremely complex and will take time to understand it. Do you want me to tell you now? I think I can't tell you now.
- Now you have to teach Hasina? How will you do it?
- Mom that is different. We have the actual work to do, and then I will teach her how to do that work and how to keep track of it and how to do it more efficiently. There, it is real work and things can be learnt easily.
- So show her well, I like her.

She had an inquisitive look at him but resisted asking him what was in her mind—"do you like her?", and changed the topic.

- Iqbal is it possible to search your father? Now you have many contacts, Allah has given you the money and you can do something? My conscious says that he is somewhere and suffering.
- We have tried everywhere it was possible. But as you desire, I will certainly talk to the company who specializes in this work. Allah will certainly listen to your prayers, and we will find him one day.

Sir, it is time for dinner. Can we serve now? The maid came and inquired.

They had a quiet dinner.

CHAPTER 45

Iqbal read the article next day in the paper. The drug racket run by an influential politician, the details of the scam, and the encounter details were not in much detail, but mentioned the name of Amanullah's office. The inquisitiveness to learn more aroused, and decided to investigate.

At the breakfast table, Iqbal told Sharifa, she was nervous and asked to find out details. Iqbal went to the office. Today he was late, and sure that Karimseth and Hasina will be there before him.

Indeed it happened; Hasina was in the office and looking at his photo lying on the table. He coughed to attract her attention, and she came to her senses. She realised being seen by Iqbal watching his photo.

- How are you? Rested well, I came with father and to be first in office is his weakness. He always comes before time. I am a late sleeper and mother never wakes me. But now things changed, I come to learn the business, and the first thing is to be well in time.
- Oh! You acquired the first principal of the business. These are extremely difficult to keep it. It requires discipline, and I am late today.
- Don't make life more difficult, I know my friends who hardly go to work but enjoy life. I don't know how they do it. I want to enjoy life and work both. Only work is boring for me.
- Then I am not the right teacher for you.
- Don't worry, you teach me the work, and I teach you how to enjoy life.

Iqbal could see the flick in Hasina's eyes. The thought of Tabassum confused him, He could not decide whether it will be relevant to introduce Tabassum and his relationship. He decided to wait and tell later.

Iqbal had the serious problem of finding Abdulla, which Sharifa wanted it. So he thought to share this with Hasina. He told her everything that Sharifa had suffered in life, and now it was most sacred purpose of his life to make her happy and find the missing father.

His phone rang, and it was Karimseth who wanted him.

- Iqbal now I plan to be relieved of my business days so that I can devout sometime to spiritual and social responsibilities. Hasina is now joining you and I am sure, she will be a significant help, Karimseth said.
- Yes, indeed, but without your supervision and involvement, I will be lost. Why are you thinking of retiring?

No, planning to perform the Haj Pilgrimage and will be away for at least two to three months. It will be an excellent opportunity for you to take charge of the business. Has Sharifa performed the Haj?

- I will certainly try my best. I am sure those three to four months is reasonable, and will manage it. Yes—my mother has not been to Haj pilgrimage, but will ask her. I don't think she will go without me, and that is not possible.
- Ok you ask her, I will be most happy if she can perform Haj with us. She has a passport, I presume.
- No, she has no passport. We can get one, if she wishes to join.
- There is an inquiry from Madras and I want you to go there, meet the client and check how we can offer the items required. It is an excellent business proposition, and you can ensure that business.
- Yes, I will do the needful, don't worry.

Iqbal noted the necessary details and walked back to office. On entering, saw Hasina with his photo and felt uncomfortable. He coughed and drew her attention. But this time Hasina's response was different.

- Iqbal, the more I watch your photo, it looks you resemble so much to your mother.
- Iqbal laughed, I am her son so what?, that is how Allah designed me.

- No, but Allah does not do the same for everybody; I don't resemble either my father or mother. I am different. So my question is why you? I was studying your photo.
- Did you get the answer?
- No, but I am thinking that your mother, who suffered so much in life and prayed that you resemble her and Allah has answered the prayers.
- It is a lousy reason that you have; I cannot question or comment on it. Now put that photo aside and discuss business. You have come here to study business and not me. I have to go to Madras and will be away for two days.
- So I come to Madras with you, it will be a part of job training too.
- Nothing doing, I cannot take you with me. You will stay here, and I will give you the work which you will finish in two days. No argument, I am a strict boss, and he laughed.
- Yes, Sir, Hasina saluted, and they both had a merry laugh.

In her laugh, Iqbal felt the resemblance of Tabassum. He was confused and frightened with what was happing in his life.

On reaching home, he informed Sharifa about the visit to Madras and he will be gone for two days. He informed Karimseth's Haj intention and asking Sharifa to join with his family.

- No, I will not go. I will go either with you or with your father. I know he is there and suffering. You have to find him.
- Yes, I am going to do that after I come back from Madras.

Iqbal left for Madras.

He had an extremely elaborate and exciting business plan from the client. The company was in South Africa and had a strong potential. Mr. Rangarajan was a charming individual. His philosophy of business was remarkably simple. Don't calculate the profit that you will gain from the business. Measure the trust and confidence of the customer. This is the first secret to an assured business.

- But how do I calculate the trust and confidence of the customer, Iqbal asked him.
- Yes, extremely easy. Be honest with him. Look in his eyes while talking. Show how you can help to meet his goal. Tell him how you

understand his needs, satisfy those needs and the glare in his eyes will tell you.

- It is not that simple.
- Yes, I know. No calculator gives you the calculations of these parameters. The calculators only calculate money not the motive. You are still at the beginning stage of your business life. It is expected that you follow this code in your active life. I know Karimseth and how he has developed the business. I wish you the same.
- I have understood the current status that you have told me. As the business is in South Africa, I will have to discuss with Karimseth and take it further.
- Yes, indeed, we have a week to respond to the client.
- Sir, we have finished our discussions. Is there time to visit interesting sites in the city? This is my first visit.
- Sure, I will ask the driver to take you around and let me check if my son Murty can join.

He called Murty, a young man and introduced him to Iqbal.

- This is his first visit. Show him the city. I don't know what he wants to see. But take care of him. He leaves early morning tomorrow so do not make it late night.
- Yes, dad I will take care.

Iqbal left the office with Murty.

- Where shall we go? What interests you? Murty asked him.
- I am open, nothing specific, you decide.
- There is Mahapalipuram, an hour's drive from South Madras. It is a heritage site along the beach. We can visit Theosophical society in Adyar a place to walk—only nature and full of trees. There is an ancient Library with antique collection of books. If you are interested in animals, we go to Guindy. Snake/crocodile park where we can watch shows of "taking the venom out of snakes". I don't enjoy.

If you want to view the beauty of Madras, we should go to Marina Beach, supposed to be exciting in ancient days, but today you have different scenes. Do you wish to see it? I am fond of going to beaches, it relaxes.

There is a Connemara Public Library. The library is supposed to have every book published in India (English) since 18th century.

One place of your interest could be Thousand lights Mosque on Mount Road. The mosque is the largest in the country and ancient.

- Let us go to library, I love books, Iqbal said.

There were interesting books and Iqbal got engrossed in it. He wanted to spend more time, but realised that this was boring for Murty.

- Let us go to the beach, he said with excitement to Murty.

On the beach, it was pleasant, and they had a long walk. Iqbal enjoyed, but Murty was silent. The crowd at the beach was not as per his expectations.

The prayer time was approaching, and there was not much time to go to the Thousand Light Mosque. Iqbal decided to go to a nearby mosque and pray. Iqbal while coming out of the mosque after prayers saw a beggar that confused him. The beggar looked decidedly much like the father. The face was full of wrinkles and a long beard. Iqbal was not sure at the first sight. He went out and met Murty waiting for him. Iqbal could not discuss what he had seen but wanted to make sure.

- He told him to wait for more time and went inside to search that person. The person had gone and not to be found anywhere. Iqbal inquired, and nobody able to help. Everyone wanted the charity, and he was paying to get the blessings of Allah.

Iqbal could not find him, nobody could help him, he returned back to Murty, and told he was not feeling well and not going to have dinner, and requested to drop him at the hotel.

Murty felt uncomfortable. What has happened to him? Why he has, lost desire to speak. He even saw a worried look on Iqbal's face.

- Hope you are alright? You look disturbed. I can help, please let me know.
- No, I thank you for your time. Now, I will be coming here more often, I keep more time for sightseeing. It is indeed a vibrant city.

He went to the hotel.

Next day morning he arrived back in Calcutta.

He was not clear what to tell Sharifa.

He decided to expand the search and explore the whole issue with the organization which he had in his mind. It was a costly affair, but the price was not a matter of concern.

Has he seen him?

Was he, his father?

Has he recognised him?

Did he run away on seeing him?

Searching his father was now of the utmost priority.

The happiness of mother was his now most sacred mission.

CHAPTER 46

Hamid was worried. The bag in the house had created fear.

Hamid had no immediate answer on what to do. He had realized that the bag must have the drugs. His confused condition remained an issue with Zaheda.

- Why are you so much tensed and stressed, Zaheda asked?
- Our life is in turmoil. We did not listen to Tabassum and now she is in the most difficult status of her life. She is a widow at the young age. The wealth, which we thought will make life happy, has gone.
- You did not listen. You wanted money, money and money.
- No, Amanullah and Ashraf had trapped me. Ashraf threatened dire consequences if I don't listen. I told you everything and Tabassum sacrificed her life. I should have gone to jail and suffered.

The telephone rang. Zaheda answered it. Caller wanted to talk to Hamid.

- It is for you.
- Who is he?
- He refused to give his name and wants to talk to you.

Hamid took the phone.

- Listen, I am coming to your house to collect the bag.
- I am sorry, who are you? What are you saying?
- Do not try to be smart with us. We are dangerous people.
- You cannot get the bag. The bag belongs to Amanullah, and I cannot give it to you

He blurted out. Zaheda was listening.

- What is it? Which bag he wants? Which bag of Amanullah is in our house? Zaheda intervened.
- Keep quiet, let me finish, and I will tell you, Hamid covered the mouthpiece and asked her to be quiet.

Hamid had blurted out the truth.

- Can I meet you somewhere and discuss this out? I am going to Amanullah's house and ask his wife.
- Nothing doing, no one knows. You will not discuss the bag with anyone. Be smart and hand it over to me.
- You have to meet me first before I do that.
- I am coming to your house, then.
- No, not now. I have guest in the house, and impossible to meet you now. Can I meet you tomorrow?
- Ok don't be smart and go to the police. The bag is full of drugs. The value of that bag is 1 crore. If you give the bag to me, you will get your share too.
- How much?

The talk of money weakened him.

- Ten lakhs.
- Ten lakhs! He could not control his excited voice.
- Yes, ten lakhs, so be smart and use your brain.

He disconnected the phone.

Zaheda heard ten lakhs, she was aware of her husband's weakness.

Zaheda recollected what happened in the past when Amanullah dragged her husband into wrong activities. She decided to find out the truth, and stop him from doing something wrong.

Hamid disconnected the phone and sat on a chair.

- Will you tell the truth? What is this? Are you involved in their wrong doing which killed them? Who was on the phone and what does he want?

She caught hold of Hamid and shook him.

Hamid had no choice but to speak out the truth.

On hearing the truth, Zaheda now understood why the pillows on the bed got interchanged. She realised why the lock was not there when Sakina visited the house. She was sure the suspected bag was under the bed.

- I am not going to allow you to meet those mafias.
- What shall we do?

- Go to police and inform. Tell the truth how the bag came to our house.
- Who will believe us? Amanullah is not there to confirm it.
- We speak the truth.
- Truth, truth, truth—who believes in it now!! They will first arrest me and put in jail. Do you want that I go to Jail? I have been once there and don't want to go there again. Your truth will put me behind the bar. Do you want it?

The fear of Hamid going to jail weakened Zaheda.

- Why did you do this in the first place?
- I was thinking of Tabassum and hoped that I am helping her family. I had no idea. What is in the bag? He never told me. It was for a week, so I thought let me help him.
- No, it was the greed of getting the cash for it. You always wanted to get money by any means.
- Yes, my weakness. I always wanted to give a diamond necklace to you but never had money. This tempted me. Now they are offering 10 lacs to me, so let them come and take the bag.
- I don't want necklace from you. Get rid of the bag from our house. I have lost my daughter because of your greed. I am happy with what I have.

The phone rang.

Zaheda wanted to pick it up, but Hamid did not allow and let it ring.

The phone stopped ringing, and the door bell rang.

Hamid was afraid to open the door. The bell continued to ring.

Zaheda decided to open the door. Hamid went away in his room. It was Sakina.

- What is wrong aunty; I have been ringing the door? The voice from inside indicated that you were in the house.
- I am sorry; I and uncle were in the middle of discussion and did not hear your bell. What is it that you want?
- I came to inform you that Tabassum is ill.
- Oh, my Allah—what is wrong with us now. Our daughter is suffering. I am going to their house.

Phone rang. Now it had to be answered as Sakina was in the house.

- Why are you not answering our call, the voice at the other end shouted?

- No everything is fine. We are OK, Hamid tried to show it as normal call from a friend.
- Stop fooling around; else you will pay a heavy price, the voice threatened.
- Not that serious, we are just leaving our house to go to Tabassum house. We will be away. We will call you after we come back.
- Idiot, what are you talking? Tell when we can come and collect the bag, the confused voice at the other end shouted.
- We are out of the house for another two hours.
- So can we come and collect the bag? Is this what you are saying?
- Yes, and we settle accounts after words, I trust you.

The greed of money was still hanging around.

- So it will be done today, and he disconnected the phone.

They left for Tabassum's house.

CHAPTER 47

Iqbal's mission was to find Abdullah.

Iqbal contacted a security service company and gave them the full details of Abdullah. He explained them the circumstances in which he had left the home. He gave the details of Madras visit and seeing a similar person in the mosque.

The security people took the details and assured that they will find him if alive. He is alive that is what my mother says, so it has to be.

- We respect her sentiments, and hope we can get him.

A fee of Rs. 50000/-, and expenses paid on actual was finalised.

Hasina, who was present during discussions, got now involved into Iqbal's personal life.

- Your life is work and work only. I told you that I will show you how to enjoy life. Today we will go to the swimming pool, and I will introduce you to my friends who enjoy life. Will you come? Hasina asked Iqbal.
- I don't know swimming. Who are they? Your friends will be girls. I cannot be comfortable with them.
- What? Don't you know swimming? It is refreshing. You must learn it, and I will teach you.
- No, I am not interested, and scared of water.
- Oh God, what is there to be scared off.? There will be a professional coach who will teach you how to swim. No arguments and we are going. I am the boss, and as I am following instructions of my boss you follow instructions of your boss. So it is final, after office we are going to the swimming pool.

- What about Karimseth? Will he approve it?
- Don't worry. I will tell him that I am teaching you how to swim. It is he who taught me how to swim since I was five years old. He is an excellent swimmer and a diver too. I cannot dive.
- What is the difference between a diver and a swimmer?
- You are a dumb when it comes to swimming. Wait and you will learn fast. You are a fantastic learner.

They were at the swimming pool.

- I will go and change. You stay here, just watch, and get acquainted with the environment.

Iqbal was looking and enjoying. Children jumping in the pool and splashing water everywhere. They had no fear of water, and life was fun. There were young girls in their bikinis and this was something embarrassing for him to look at them. The waiter came and asked him if he needed something to drink. There was imported wine, and he will enjoy it.

- I don't drink; just get a lemon juice.

Iqbal saw Hasina in bikini, and the towel wrapped around her. Hasina came closer, and called the waiter and ordered a pair of sandwich and a beer.

- What! You drink beer! Iqbal could not control the tone of his voice. It is not allowed in our religion. I am going away; I cannot sit here and drink with you. Does your father know this? He will get upset, and you will lose your love and respect.
- I am sorry if I hurt your religious sentiments. I am not that religious, but I don't drink every day. It is with friends when we have fun days, I enjoy it. I honestly cannot understand why we can't drink it. She called the waiter and cancelled the order of beer and opted for the lemon juice.

She got up, dropped her towel on the chair and jumped into the water. Iqbal was stunned looking at her. He had never seen a young girl in a bikini. She had a lovely shape and sexy appeal. He got lost in the thought of what she means by this display of her body and what is the reason she brought him to the swimming pool. What about the drink? He was enjoying the environment and the surroundings and never wanted to come out of it.

After few minutes, she came out. Her body now drenched with dripping water. She grabbed the towel and wrapped it. This happened in few seconds, but the effect on Iqbal was immense.

The waiter came with the order.

- So what do you think? You wish to learn swimming. There is a teacher. I can call him, and we can fix up everything. You get dedicated to swimming as you are in your work and you learn faster.
- Let me think. But I enjoy here and interested to learn swimming.
- You will not discuss with my father what has happened here I cannot understand what is wrong in beer. It is a refreshing drink. Let us be loyal friends and keep our secrets with us.
- Will you still drink?
- I cannot tell you now. I am thinking.

Hasina saw friend Tehmina and Tara entering the pool.

- Hi how are you? They looked at Iqbal with mischievous intent and looked back at Hasina with a smile.
- This is Iqbal, manager of our exports division. I am learning the business ethics. So how are you? Where is Yasmin? Is she not with you today?
- Oh she had work and did not come today. We are sure you enjoy good fun. Bye then.

Iqbal was just watching.

- We will now go, he spoke.
- Why you don't want to meet the teacher and decide on your learning.
- I think give me the time to decide. How many days will it take to learn?
- If your mother had thrown you in the pool at the age of five as my father did, today you would have been an excellent swimmer.
- Yes, indeed, easy to say. You have no idea what my mother had to endure in life. Your childhood was fun. You had a loving father. Well let us go and not spoil our pleasant moments.
- I am sorry, I hurt your feelings, please forgive me. She caught hold of Iqbal. Her hand brought a chill in his body. He let her continue to hold it.

Was the life opening another chapter for him?

CHAPTER 48

Iqbal was now in mental conflict.

Is Hasina in love with him?

Is he in love with her?

He decided to resolve the issue by having a frank discussion with her.

- Iqbal, you don't have a good circle of friends. Why is it so? Mumbai's life is so hectic, fun and friends. Calcutta is dull, and people are reserved. Mumbai, we heard is always exciting and fun, Hasina said

- My life in Mumbai was simple and limited. I never had money to spend with friends. My mother was working hard to keep the family running. Education was the top most priority. There was no need of friends and I had one very good friend and never needed more.

- So you had at least one friend, you were not alone. What is he doing now? Are you in touch with him?

- It is not he. It is she.

- Oh, so you had a girl friend.

- I had a friend who was a girl.—I never had a girl friend.

- Something new, new definitions, very interesting.

- Can you tell me more? Can I meet her? Where is she? Are you in touch with her?

- No, I am not in touch with her now. Her father got her married against her will.

- Married? Against her will, what a father he is? I will never do it. I will run away from the house.

- These are thoughts, but difficult to execute. Life is not that simple. I honestly don't know what made her agree to her father. It is a mystery to me till now. We had a lovely childhood. We shared many things. She never shared with me her difficult decision to get married.

- It is indeed sad, do you still remember her?
- Yes, she is a part of my life. I cannot forget her.
- But you will get married soon, and you will love your wife.
- I am not going to get married.
- What are you talking? Why this crucial decision? You never loved her.
- After that difficult decision of her life, I started loving her. She never realised it. I wanted to run away with her, but my mother was my top most priority. My aunt had run away. You know, my father, left us deserted. I could not do it to my mother.
- If you had proposed, would she run away with you?
- I told you, because of my mother and the circumstances which were prevailing in our house, I just did not think it was right for me to run away.
- But your mother is now preparing for your marriage. Every mother wants son to get married. Will you disappoint her?
- I have not thought. I will do it when the time comes. Let us not bother too much. I have work to do. You know my visit to South Africa.

Though the issue discontinued, Hasina felt disturbed. The life of Iqbal had many problems and frustrations. This started to bother her.

How can I help him?

How can I bring happiness in his life?

I like him; I think I am in love with him.

How can I create those feelings in him?

Does he still love Tabassum, though she is married now?

Sir, is calling you, the office boy came and brought her away from her dream.

Please arrange the details of the South African Customer in proper order. The list of our contacts and suppliers who can meet client's requirements.

- It is arranged and ready.
- Excellent?
- Yes, by now I know how you work and I keep myself prepared.
- You are indeed a good help in my work.
- I can be a good help to you in life too.

Iqbal looked at her, she was smiling. He responded and both laughed.

- I will remember that Hasina, he replied.
- When are you going? She inquired.
- I think it will be on Monday.

The desk phone rang. The receptionist told him that the security man has come and wants to meet.

Send him, he told the receptionist.

The man came with the photographs.

- Our representative in Madras had visited the mosque you had informed. He has ten photographs of the people matching your description. Look at it sir.

Iqbal looked at the photographs.

- I am not sure, these three looks alike. Let my mother see. Leave them here. I will check with her and inform.
- I am coming home with you, Hasina said.

They went home and showed the photographs to Sharifa.

- This is him, Iqbal, this is him. He is alive. My son, go and bring him home.

She could not control her excitement.

She could not control her emotions.

She cried and fainted.

Hasina ran to the kitchen to get water. Iqbal wanted to call the doctor.

- Don't worry she is excited. It is an emotional issue, and she will be alright. But still call the doctor.
- Iqbal went to phone the doctor.

Sharifa was in Hasina's lap. She opened the eyes.

- When can you bring him home? Where is he? Can I come with you?
- Mom, How sure you are?
- Yes, I am sure. He is my husband. Where is he?
- He is in the mosque at Madras where I had a glimpse of him. Before I could meet him, he went away.
- Then go and bring him.
- Mom, I am leaving for South Africa and everything is planned. I will be returning after a week. We will then take care of him. Since we

located him, now he cannot go anywhere. There will somebody who will watch him and keep track.

- What? She shouted. He is your father. Allah has sent him back and you want to go for your business trip. Are you not ashamed of this?
- She is right, Hasina intervened. Postpone the business trip and they will understand. Your priority is your father and not your business.
- Mom, I am sorry, forgive me. I will go to Madras tomorrow and bring him home.
- I want to come with you.
- No, my request is that let me go alone. What do you think Hasina?
- Yes, let Iqbal go alone. I will stay here with you, and we do our prayers for his safe return.

Karimseth was informed about this happy event. He agreed to postpone the South Africa trip and Iqbal left for Madras.

The security man advised him to be away from the car. He will go alone and bring the identified person to the car.

The mosque was full of people. Iqbal wanted to go for prayers, but security people advised him to go to a different mosque to avoid any suspicion and confusion if he sees him there. Iqbal never wanted to take a chance on this. He agreed and went away.

After the prayer, one of the security men who had pretended to be a beggar moved near to Abdullah.

- In that car, a lady is distributing food and gives Rs.10 in charity. Let us go and get it. He told two more beggars, and they moved towards the car. They got their share and moved away.

When Abdullah went near the car, Iqbal caught hold of him. Iqbal removed his scarf and told

- Papa, I am your son Iqbal. Look at me.

Abdullah could not believe it.

- Iqbal hugged him; I have come to take you. Mom is waiting and praying for you. Let us go home, our life problems are resolved. Allah has given me everything. He has even given back you too. He has forgiven us, and you don't have to worry.

Abdullah was silent. He cried and hugged Iqbal.

- How is Sharifa? Will she forgive me?
- There is no forgiving in the family. I am happy that I got you back. She is waiting for you. She is in Calcutta where we stay.
- Calcutta? Did you come from Calcutta?

- Yes, I was in Madras fifteen days ago and saw you in the mosque but was not sure. By the time I came back, you went away. Did you recognise me then?
- No, I did not. I must have gone, and you came back.

The crowd had gathered. The security man wanted to move away from the place as fast as he can.

He requested them to get in the car. Iqbal led Abdullah to the car, and they moved out. They went to the hotel where required arrangements were made. Abdullah had a bath, haircut, and he refused to remove the beard. He had a simple but dignified dress.

Iqbal requested Abdullah to offer prayers. Abdullah did the same.

They had an evening flight. At Calcutta airport, Karimseth and Hasina were there to welcome him. Abdullah shocked to see the changes in the life of his son. He inquired about Sharifa.

- She is waiting at home and will meet you there, Iqbal said.

They reached home. She came running to meet Abdullah but could not hug him in the presence of everybody.

- Please forgive me, Abdullah could not speak further. His voice was chocked.

Karimseth had instructed that no one should ask Abdullah any questions. Iqbal gave the progress of his life and how Karimseth had helped him in life.

Karimseth refused to accept any credit for the progress of Iqbal. It was his effort and it was Allah's blessings.

It was the end of the day. Every one left. Abdullah wanted to tell them how and what he had suffered, but not allowed to speak. Forget everything and look forward.

- You have suffered enough, so now take rest, do your prayers and enjoy the life, Iqbal said.
- Where is Shabana? He asked
- We don't know, but the last news we have had from Himmat uncle was that they are in Dubai. I don't know.
- Can we find them?
- I don't know, but they are happy, so let them be happy. You now go and take rest.

Sharifa and Abdullah were alone.

They looked at each other. They could not speak. The sufferings had taken over them. Abdullah held Sharifa's hand.

- Forgive me for what I have done to you. You are my Angel, and I pray to Allah to bless you for what you gave me and punish me for what I did to you.
- I have forgiven you. The proof is Allah has given you back to me.

They held their hands for a long time and went to sleep.

CHAPTER 49

On reaching Tabassum's home, Hamid and Zaheda found that she was down with typhoid. Doctor advised that she should be admitted to hospital, but as she was under the religious mourning period and cannot leave the house. They explained to the doctor that being a married woman, the religion has imposed an isolation period of 4 month 15 days. This is to ascertain if she is pregnant. Her pregnancy would be known by that time. This gives protection to her, ascertains the father and avoids controversies. The doctors understood and appreciated the situation, but medical care was must for her. Zaheda wanted to appoint a full time nurse and a daily visit of the doctor to avoid any complications. Hamid consulted maulvis to find a solution. Maulvis advised there was nothing wrong in her breaking the mourning period if that was the question of her life. The protection of life gets priority. This was a relief to the family.

Zaheda wanted to stay and look after Tabassum. This was acceptable to the family, but Tabassum was not willing. The death of Amanullah and Ashraf had given a serious jolt to the family. Their pride, prestige and privileges of life already lost, and were now more humble. They requested Zaheda not to stress, and they will take care of Tabassum.

On returning home, they found the house in shambles. Somebody entered the house and ransacked it. Hamid realised that the bag was removed from the house and had lost 10 Lacs of Rupees.

- I am sure of your involvement with them and in trouble again. You will not tell me anything. You ruined the life of Tabassum. Allah will never forgive. Zaheda lost her patience.

Hamid caught hold of her hand and made her sit on the chair. He told everything to her from the day Amanullah called him and asked him to keep the bag in the house. He had no choice but to help him as he was the relative.

Zaheda heard everything. She started arranging the things in the house. Nobody had noticed anything, and the incident remained between them. Hamid was in prayers. He was sure his problems are finished. He prayed and asked the forgiveness, promised to be a devoted husband and a loving father.

Days passed. Tabassum recovered and was in better spirits. Once the mourning period ends, she decided to pursue her ambition of life and become a doctor. She wanted to meet Iqbal.

The government officials were waiting for the period of mourning to be over to take possession of the house. They came and served the notice. Fifteen days extension granted, and the family asked to move out.

Tabassum came back to her house. She was now free to move and do her normal routine. Hamid was a changed person. He was seeking the forgiveness from the daughter.

- Mom, I want to meet Iqbal, Do you have his address or the number so that I can contact him, and she asked Zaheda.
- No, I do not have anything. He went to stay with his grandfather. Sharifa came here once to receive Iqbal when he was coming from Calcutta, where he is working. They stayed for two days and left. We have no contact with them. The house is locked.

Tabassum was nervous but not disheartened. Her conscious was telling her that she will find him, she will meet him, and she will resolve all the issues of life with him. He is a friend whom she can always trust.

She decided to put an advertisement in the paper.

The advertisement read

"Iqbal, I am looking for you. Iqbal, I need you. Iqbal, if you see this ad contact me.—You are aware where to contact me."

She was sure; the right Iqbal will find a way to meet her.

Sakina helped her to put the advertisement in the paper as they needed all the details of the advertiser.

For the next three days, the advertisement came in the paper. There was no response.

Iqbal was in South Africa.

Hasina read the ad, and was wondering if she is Tabassum. As there was no contact address or number given, she was helpless. Hasina contacted the newspaper office to find out if they can give the contact address or number of the advertiser, but they refused as it was against the policy. It was left for Iqbal to come and decide.

Iqbal came after a week.

Hasina was anxious to meet him at the earliest opportunity. Iqbal was held up in long meetings with Karimseth, and other business associates.

At the end of the day, she caught hold of him.

- Read this ad in the paper, published a week ago.
- Leave it, I am now tired and would like to go home and be with my parents.
- Yes, but crucial. Someone is looking for you.
- For me?
- Yes, I think so. You read it and tell me if I am right.

Iqbal read the ad. He was thrilled to learn Tabassum was looking for him.

- What do I do, Hasina? I feel the same, she needs me.
- Do not have any contact of her?
- No, I do not have. When I left last time from Mumbai, she had told me to get out of her life. She told me not to attend her marriage. She wanted to forget me. In my frustration, I also left everything in Mumbai and came here.
- Please think about something. I am confused, and I would like to go and spend the time with my mother.
- I have an idea. You also put an ad in the paper and give your contact details. If she reads, she will contact. Yes, you are right, we do it tomorrow. Will you organise it for me?
- Yes, I will.

Next day the Ad came in the paper.

"I am Iqbal, contact me on 25786786."—The Ad was quite bold and located on three pages, and to be released for the week.

The response came on the very first day. Hasina's thinking had worked.

- Can I speak to Mr. Iqbal? I am responding in response to the advertisement inserted in today's paper.
- You identify yourself first. These are strict instructions, the telephone operator responded.
- Tell him, I am Sakina and he will talk to me.

The message conveyed to Iqbal and Hasina took the phone.

- Yes, please tell me what you wish to say, Hasina asked.
- Who are you? My name is Sakina, and I was his neighbour in Mumbai before he moved to Calcutta.

- Please wait, I will speak to him.

Iqbal thought it was Sakina. He took the phone.

- Iqbal, Iqbal and the voice crumbled.

You are Tabassum! I cannot forget your voice. How are you? It is a long time we spoke. Where are you and when can I meet you?

- I also want to meet you. When can you come to Mumbai? I now stay with my parents.
- Why?
- It is a tragedy of my life. Meet me and I tell you everything. I want to tell you everything, and I also want to know everything about you. How is my mom Sharifa?

She could not control her emotions, and started crying.

- Give me your telephone no, Iqbal asked.
- She gave, and Hasina noted it
- Taboo, I found my father. He is now with us.

Unable to control his excitement, Iqbal shared with her the biggest success of his life.

- Ok, I am coming to Mumbai and will meet you on Sunday, Iqbal said.
- What you found him? Sharifa aunt's prayers answered by Allah. Allah always answers her prayers. Come soon, I am waiting for you.

Hasina could notice the intensity of emotions on the face of Iqbal.

She realised Iqbal's desire for Tabassum.

She realised Tabassum's desire for Iqbal.

She wanted to meet her at the earliest.

- Iqbal can I come with you to Mumbai, I want to meet her.

I cannot tell Hasina, but we go home and talk to my mother. I am planning to take both of them and even call my Nana and Nani to Mumbai so that my father can meet them.

- It is a good idea then my coming will not be a hassle for me.
- Our house is small; you may have to sleep in the kitchen.
- With you, I can sleep anywhere.

She closed the door and ran away.

Iqbal was confused.

Iqbal gave the news of talking with Tabassum to Sharifa and Abdullah. He also informed them about the plans to go to Mumbai. Call Nana and Nani to Mumbai, and then we bring them to Calcutta. He also informed Sharifa about Hasina's coming with them, and got the silent approval from her.

They all left for Mumbai.

It was a happy occasion for everyone, and they all came to meet Sharifa and Abdullah. A changed Abdullah was the main attraction for the visitors. Masood, Shirin and Hussain also came. Hamid, Zaheda impressed by the tremendous change in the stature of Iqbal.

There was no privacy for Tabassum to talk to Iqbal. They were simply surrounded by the visitors. The day was coming to an end, and visitors started going back. Hamid and Zaheda also said goodbye. Hamid's guilt was visible and expressed in his humble talk with Iqbal. Iqbal also responded with dignity, and did not make him uncomfortable at all.

- Mom, I need to talk to Iqbal and will come little later, Tabassum said to Zaheda.
- They all must be tired, let them rest, and tomorrow you can talk. I invited them for dinner tomorrow. Sharifa has accepted the invitation.
- As, you wish. Iqbal, I am going, and tomorrow I need to listen to all what you did and achieved.
- Ya, we will talk tomorrow then. I report to you else I get my punishment. Iqbal laughed. Tabassum also laughed, but the charm of that smile was missing.

Hasina was observing all this and wondering.

In the morning after breakfast, Hasina took Iqbal aside.

- Tell me all about you and Tabassum. I must know it.
- What is there to know? I already told you that she is my childhood friend. We shared the best moments of our life. We enjoyed it, and have deep respect for each other.
- Did you love her? Did she love you?
- Yes, we both loved each other as a friend.
- No, I mean as a man and woman. The way I love you.
- What non-sense. Are you mad? I cannot love you. You are the daughter of my boss. The man who changed my destiny. I am not going to betray his trust in me.
- There is nothing wrong in loving the boss's daughter if you wish to marry and accept as a wife.
- You are mad. How this thought ever came into your mind?
- No, I am not. I am in love with you, and that is the reason I came here to see myself and find out the truth.
- And what truth did you find out?
- I think, she loves you, and she wants to marry you.

- How do you know?
- I am a woman, and I do feel how it is. Can we all three meet somewhere outside and discuss it out? I don't want to come in your way. I loved you and did not get your love is my destiny. I am not the one, who cribbles about it. I want to be frank, and if need be I will go away from your life.
- Hasina, please do not be too sentimental. There is nothing between me and Tabassum.
- Then do you love me. Will you marry me?
- I can't tell you. My mother will decide about it. Please close this topic and let us be good friends.

Sharifa walked in and looked at both of them. You both are in the serious discussions. Why so serious?

- No mom, nothing. Did you all sleep well?
- We are invited for dinner by Zaheda, and we are going there, you are aware about it.
- Yes, but now we are going out for lunch.
- Where and why? Be with us.
- Mom, you know Tabassum. We are going for jalebis. You will not allow me to eat it, and he laughed.
- He eats lot of sweets. All because Tabassum loves sweets. I am still surprised that she has not changed that habit, Sharifa laughed and said to Hasina.

Iqbal had created this so that they all three are out and Hasina and Tabassum can understand each other better.

They were all sitting in a posh restaurant.

- Why we came here? Can we get those jalebis here? Tabassum said.
- Yes, you will, much better than your oily jalebis. I will not need your shalwar then to clean my hands, Iqbal laughed.

Hasina could not understand but smiled too.

- Will you excuse me, I go to the washroom, Iqbal said, and went.

He wanted to be away so that the two can be alone, and Hasina can talk it out with Tabassum.

- You are very pretty, this dress is good and goes well on you, Tabassum said,
- Thank you but you are also very sweet looking and charming.
- You are being polite. I am a widow, and had a distressing marriage.
- Did you love Iqbal?

- Yes, since childhood, but never thought of marrying him till I was being forced into marriage by my father. Then I did thought of him as my lover, my husband and even proposed to him. I was even willing to run away with him, but it was not my destiny. I forgot about it, and I want him back in my life as my friend. I need him.
- He loves you too and wants to marry you.
- Don't be silly. Did he tell you that? Is this the reason why he has called me here? Has he asked you to tell me this?
- No, but I am asking.
- Why?
- Because, I love him. I want to marry him.

Tabassum rattled by this open confession.

- He is all yours. I will not spoil his life by asking him to marry me. I am his well wisher. I like you too. You are lucky to have him as a husband. Promise me that you will not take him away from me. I want him as my friend; I need him as my guide for the remaining journey of my life. Promise me, please promise, me please,

She caught Hasina's hands as if she was begging.

Iqbal walked and saw them in a serious discussion. He saw wetness in the eyes of Tabassum.

- You people still not decided to order anything. I am hungry, he said.
- Yes, we already decided something. You are a lucky man. We both decided to marry you. I am your first wife and she is your second. You still have two more options, because you are allowed four by the religion. For the third you take her permission.
- Lucky man! Are you crazy! What joke and fun is this? Please order food; let us enjoy our meals and go.

He ordered the meal and they all enjoyed it. It was Tabassum all the way talking and narrating all the fun she had. Hasina and Iqbal were listening.

- I am finished, now it is your turn to say what you did and how you did it. How did you find your father? How you fell in love with Hasina? How could you forget me?

It was the old Tabassum now getting back to her mischief, back to her teasing of Iqbal. The glimpse of her missing smile was also back.

- I will tell you everything. Wait for some time. Let's go. I have lot of work to do. Let me tell you one thing—you are not forgotten. I can never forget you. He caught hold of Tabassum's hand and started moving out.

CHAPTER 50

At home, Hussain discussed with Masood and Shirin,

- What about Iqbal's marriage.?
- Yes, now is the right time. He is doing well. Sharifa needs help and company of a woman in the house. Abdullah is there now and by the grace of Allah, the life is settled.
- Karimseth likes Iqbal and is keen to make him, his family member. He has indicated to me about Hasina. He made sure by putting Hasina in the office with Iqbal so that they acquaint each other better.
- No doubt, she is pretty, and I am sure Iqbal will accept her.

They asked Sharifa and Abdullah to join them and informed what Hussain said about Hasina and Karimseth's view point. They wished and prayed that it will happen.

Iqbal, Tabassum, and Hasina entered the room.

Iqbal was holding the hand of Tabassum. They saw it and got confused.

- A good lunch. We enjoyed it. Hope you all could have joined us.
- No uncle, he is not telling the truth. No good jalebis. Tasty jalebis are available in our Mohalla. Tabassum laughed and said.
- For you, Jalebis, always jalebis, Sharifa joined the fun.
- Ya, but Rasagullas were tasty, and I did enjoy it. You know aunty Iqbal has become well mannered, he used the hotel napkin to wipe the hands, she said, with a smile.
- Sharifa unable to control herself, laughed heartily. Nobody understood the conversation and looked at Sharifa. They never saw Sharifa laughing so whole heartedly.

- Iqbal, I want to talk to you in private. Can we go into your study room, Hussain asked.
- Sure, uncle but is it urgent?
- Yes, because I leave tomorrow and again tonight we are busy with dinner at Hamid's house.
- As you wish.

In the room Hussain said,

- We decided about your marriage. Any girl in your mind, do tell us, and we finalise the same.
- I would say no. Wait for another two years and let me get settled.
- You are well settled by the grace of Allah. Sharifa is anxious for your marriage, and she asked me to discuss it with you.
- I still will ask and convince her to delay it. I am sure she will listen to me.
- So you don't want to fulfil her wish.
- I did not say that, but I will make her understand, and she will fulfil my wish.
- Now tell me about Hasina? Do you like her?
- Hasina? Not even in my dreams. She is the daughter of a rich father and I am sure they would not like to give their daughter to a poor man like me.
- Let me tell you. Karimseth likes you very much. It is he, who has initiated the whole issue and has given me this responsibility. Will you refuse him? Karimseth is the man, who has changed your life, who has given you so much happiness. He is the man through whom you got the respect in the society. Will you deny him?

Silent Iqbal had no answer. He walked out of the room and went to Sharifa.

- Mom, what Hussain uncle is saying to me? Are you aware of it? Do you want me to get married to Hasina?

Sharifa nodded in silence.

- Where is Tabassum? He inquired.
- She and Hasina are in the next room.
- Have you told them? Is Hasina aware about this?
- No, we have not, but we don't know if Hasina has been told by her father.

Iqbal left and went to the other room. Hasina and Tabassum sitting on a rocking chair were humming a song.

- Why are you so excited? Are you getting married? Asked Tabassum.

A bombshell for Iqbal.

It means that everyone is aware. He looked at Hasina. She was composed and quite as usual. She continued her humming.

- Yes, everyone in the family wants that I should get married.
- Did they find the girl then?
- Yes, they have found one. You know Inayatullah, that Jalebi maker. It is his daughter Sophia. I will now have jalebis every day, irritated Iqbal said.
- It is fantastic. I know her. A bit fatty but Ok, she will feed you jalebis every day, Tabassum teased him.
- But how can they do it? My mother knows that I wanted to marry you and could not. Now that the problem is solved, and I can marry you. Iqbal bent on teasing her.

On hearing, this Hasina's humming stopped.

Tabassum came near to Iqbal and slapped him. Got hold of Iqbal and said,

- My life is ruined. I am now a widow and not going to ruin your life. I will now start my study and become a doctor. You desired that I should be a doctor. My father ruined my life. Now, I want to be a doctor. I will not allow anyone to ruin my life. Not even you. You idiot, not Sophia, but Hasina is the lucky one. My conscious tells me. She is the perfect wife for you. Accept her and you will be the happiest person on earth.

Tabassum caught the hand of Hasina and gave it to Iqbal. She is yours and take care of her. Hasina loves you, make her happy.

- Tabassum ran inside and told everyone. Iqbal is ready to marry Hasina, so let us get jalebis.

The mischievous, smiling Tabassum was back.

Sharifa embraced her. Hasina ran away. Shocked Iqbal, faced a difficult time.

Hussain pleased with the decision of Iqbal greeted Masood and Shirin. They were excited and embraced Iqbal.

Tabassum brought sweets and distributed to everyone. To Hasina she gave with her own hands. Her words and actions removed all fear and worries from Hasina's mind. She prayed for her, asking Allah to bless her.

Karimseth was informed, the preparation for the marriage was on the way. They wanted to do it as soon as possible. Karimseth's family had planned their Haj travels. Iqbal desired that Sharifa and Abdullah should join, and they agreed.

Though Karimseth did not believe in elaborate marriage ceremony, he still had to do it as per the social status.

Nikah ceremony performed in the mosque. When two witnesses came to ask Hasina as per the religious norms, she said, "Qabool Hai—I agree", Tabassum got up embraced her and distributed Rasagullas to all the ladies present.

A simple but well organised reception attended by the business associates and social leaders. They all blessed the newlyweds. Hasina wore the dress of Maimuna which Sharifa requested, and she agreed. Iqbal as usual in his white Sherwani with a matching embroidery as per Hasina's wedding dress.

The guests started moving out and now it was time for the bride and groom to go. They moved towards the car. The decorated car being simple and in line with the other decorations. Tabassum joined them in the car. She being the best friend of Hasina led them to wedding room. Sharifa had entrusted her with this specific responsibility.

The cake cutting ceremony performed at the house. Tabassum led a group of young girls to sing the famous wedding song and organised a lively dance party.

She led Hasina and Iqbal to their wedding room. It was her time, now to joke and make fun of them. She remembered her wedding night, her sister-in-law, how she behaved with her killing all her pleasures.

The experience of her wedding night and the eyes became moist.

She shaked herself and got out of the mood.

- So here you are Hasina. Don't make it easy for him. Take your revenge.

The mischievous Tabassum was teasing Iqbal in his new life too.

- Wait a moment, she told Iqbal. This is a special packet which I am giving you. Open after I leave. Don't worry, I am not giving you the book which I had given. You don't need it. The whole encyclopaedia is before you.

Confused Hasina wondering what is happening. She was disturbed but pleased too.

Iqbal pushed Tabassum to the door.

- I am going but one final demand. Wait till I become a doctor. I want to deliver your first child.

She ran away and closed the door.

Iqbal came close to Hasina. He lifted her veil and looked. She was indeed looking beautiful. She closed her eyes. Iqbal could not resist. He held her and kissed her. It was his first feel of her body. After releasing her, he remembered the packet given by Tabassum. He was sure it will be all the photos of the book.

Hasina came closer to him.

Iqbal opened the jewellery box.

Box contained a diamond necklace.

There was a note. It read, "For the wife of Iqbal—by Maimuna"

The sentence revealed many things to Iqbal. He put the necklace around Hasina's neck. Looked at her with eyes full of desires. He could no longer control himself. He pulled her close and put off the lights.

A baby Tabassum was on the way.